THE LAST GUN

The railroads were opening the west, and men had to change with the times . . . or die. But Jim Regan wasn't ready to change . . . and he wasn't ready to die. His whole life had been spent pushing mule-drawn wagons of necessary supplies to towns that were separated by far distances and by great danger. Regan could not give up the only way of life he had known . . . so he had come to Silver City, to New Mexico, to a town loaded with trouble, and Regan found himself smack in the middle of a shooting war with Apaches . . . and a personal war against a man who had sworn to see him dead!

First Linford Edition
published March 1990

Copyright © 1962 by Lee Floren
All rights reserved

LEE FLOREN

THE LAST GUN

Complete and Unabridged

LINFORD
Leicester

British Library CIP Data

Floren, Lee, 1910–
   The last gun.—Large print ed.—
Linford western library
I. Title
813'.52[F]

ISBN 0-7089-6806-6

Published by
F. A. Thorpe (Publishing) Ltd.
Anstey, Leicestershire

Set by Rowland Phototypesetting Ltd.
Bury St. Edmunds, Suffolk
Printed and bound in Great Britain by
T. J. Press (Padstow) Ltd., Padstow, Cornwall

Prologue

THE LAST GUN is based on actual New Mexico history. There was indeed such a man as Jim Regan, although Jim Regan, of course, is not his real name, and this man whom I call Jim Regan did drive two hundred mules from the Black Hills of South Dakota to Silver City, Territory of New Mexico, in the year of Our Lord 1879.

And in the old mining town of Silver City this man whom I call Jim Regan did indeed meet the opposition of a town and a certain class of people and a certain strong young man—and he also met the most insidious ailment of humanity, racial bias. And through hard work and much struggle Jim Regan conquered this ancient mining town and its unfavourable peoples and he won and coveted the friendship of a certain strong young man —and he also defeated racial discrimination.

Jim Regan was, indeed, one of those fortunate men who helped advance the westward frontiers of a great nation and today his name is respected and revered in the pages of the history of the State of New Mexico.

But the author of fiction—although he hopes and attempts to follow history each patient step by step—sometimes cannot attain this perfect goal. History in many cases is not drama and history many times does not follow the course of drama— therefore it is the duty of the author of fiction to bend history into drama.

This I have laboured to do.

The dust rises . . .

Lee Floren

1

JIM REGAN left Old Wad and the Mexican and the two hundred mules at Cuchillo and rode south along the Rio Grande alone. This New Mexico Territory was a new land—a country of scarp mountains and high deserts —and he wanted to get its feel and mood. The second day found him at the base of the Pinos Altos Mountains and he turned his tired horse due west toward Silver City, knowing that Silver City would see his final stand as a freighter.

For Silver City—of all the big mining towns left in the west—was as yet the only one without a railroad.

Morning of the third day found him hiding on the side of a mountain watching a war-party of Apache braves burn three freight wagons on the floor of the desert below.

As usual, the Apaches left nothing living behind them.

Finally the Apaches left, riding into the mountains, and Regan rode on, not going down to the wreckage. There was no use.

Fatigue showed in Regan's thin, dark face. The trail down from the Black Hills of South Dakota had been long and dusty, the mules ugly and cantankerous. But he pushed this gnawing weariness to one side as he finally rode down Bullard Street, Silver City's main drag.

His blood quickened. Here lived many people—at least five thousand, he judged. These people would need supplies. Everything that came into this town came in by freight wagon.

Up on the mountain stamp mills groaned and clattered as they changed raw New Mexico ore into ingots of gold and silver. Silver ingots were piled high in front of the Bank of New Mexico.

People hurried back and forth across Bullard Street. He catalogued them—peon mine workers who lived in miserable adobe shacks, *Americano* engineers and

2

miners, bosses of the peons, housewives and storekeepers and hangerons in saloons. This was a boom town. His blood quickened.

But he was a freighter born to slow-turning high wheels, to the jerkline, to straining and sweaty mules or horses. And, because of his trade, his eyes sought out that which interested him the most—a freight depot. This he found on the west side of Bullard.

It covered half a block, a huge building made of adobe with a red tile Spanish roof. It was broken in the middle by a wide archway. Through this archway, he knew, lumbered laden freight wagons, heading for the compound and barns and living quarters in the rear, hidden by the rambling building.

Over this archway hung a sign:

NEW MEXICO WAGONS
SILVER CITY, TERRITORY OF
NEW MEXICO
JUAN de CORDOVA MARIA de
CORDOVA

There was a bench in the shade on the sidewalk. A tall young man—taller even than Regan—sat there. Regan moved his horse close. He judged this man to be about thirty. He was slender, dark-skinned, plainly of Spanish extraction. Despite the heat he wore a neat blue suit complete with vest and silk shirt and tie. His boots were polished to a high sheen.

Regan reined close to the sidewalk. "Where's your boss?"

Sharp dark eyes probed him. "Who do you mean?" The dark-skinned man spoke in rapid Spanish.

Regan glanced again at the sign. Something about this man irritated him. He tried to put a mental finger on this. Then it came to him. This man spoke to him with the scorning indifference a high-born Castillian Spaniard uses when he talks to a low peon, a mestizo.

"Juan de Cordova."

"I am Senor de Cordova."

Regan told about the Apaches. "There was no use riding down. I watched through glasses. They butchered the mules and toted the meat with them. They threw the three skinners into the flames."

De Cordova nodded. "I see. . . ."

"Just thought I'd tell you. Your wagons?"

"Not mine."

Regan frowned. "There another freight office in town?"

"There is no other. We de Cordovas have freighted in and out of Silver City for at least a hundred years. Before my sister and I owned New Mexico Wagons, my father owned it—and before him my grandfather."

Regan felt a stab of fear. Inside of him a slow bell of doom sounded, its tone sending the first touch of alarm through his blood.

Their eyes met and held.

Jim Regan spoke slowly. "So they weren't your wagons. They weren't your mules and skinners. There is no other freight outfit in Silver City. Then whose wagons and mules and skinners would they be?"

5

"I don't know," Juan de Cordova looked at his highly-polished boots. Regan saw this was only pretence for the man studied him under lidded lazy eyes. "And I don't care."

Regan dismounted slowly, the bell louder now. He stood on the boot-worn plank sidewalk.

"Three men died under Apache rifles and war-axes," he said slowly. "Sure—they're not your wagons, or your men. But you don't seem a damn' bit interested. Not even enough to get the law—or notify the soldiers at Fort Bayard?"

"None of Juan de Cordova's business."

Regan shrugged and reached to gather the reins to take his horse to the livery. De Cordova had lifted his eyes now and they still held the low esteem of a grandee of Castillian blood giving orders to a Mexican peon.

"You're the one who seems worried," de Cordova said.

Regan halted. "Am I?" His blue eyes met the dark eyes. The bell had stopped tolling—these might have been some of the wagons he'd ordered ahead through the mail from El Paso, one hundred and fifty miles southeast. They might not have been—but there was always that chance. Ramosa, the wagonmaker there, might have sent these three across the desert to Silver City, thinking he was already in town with his mules. If they had been his wagons, he was out three wagons. If so, he'd suffered a tough loss even before getting started.

"Si."

"The blood of three men means nothing, then, to you?"

De Cordova laughed silently. "They were not my men. My skinners follow the old Espejo Trail, not the Mimbres. Only a fool would travel the Mimbres Trail with Apacheris on the battle-path."

"I just came over it, so I must be a fool."

"If the boot fits—wear it."

It was not so much what de Cordova said. It was the way he said it. Regan let the reins fall and one step took him to de

7

Cordova. His right hand, twisted in the man's tie and shirt, lifted de Cordova, who had eyes of inky stern blackness. Regan heard cloth tear with silken smoothness.

De Cordova said, "Take your hands off me, you Americano dog!" He swung a right but missed for Regan had pushed him back onto the bench and had stepped back. Regan rubbed his palm on his pants as though he'd touched something dirty. De Cordova came to his feet, fists balled at his sides.

Now from the doorway came a woman's stern voice. "What is the matter out here between you two?" She spoke English with a slight Spanish accent.

She was small, not more than five feet, and she wore a buckskin riding-skirt and a white blouse. Regan saw a round small face with black snapping eyes, a full mouth, a nose slightly puggish, and a wealth of red hair, glistening with facets of sunlight. You seldom saw a red-headed Mexican woman. Rubias, the Mexicans called them, and appraised them highly.

8

Regan guessed, without being told, he was facing Maria de Cordova.

"Not a thing, hermana," de Cordova said. He did not look at his sister. He kept his eyes on Jim Regan.

Regan stepped back, bowing slightly. He said quietly, "I'm sorry, senorita." He looked at Juan de Cordova. The man was smoothing his tie, fumbling with his torn shirt.

"I could hear you in the office," Maria de Cordova said. "Who are you, stranger?"

"Just a stranger," Regan said, and left.

He walked through the dust leading his horse, a feeling of raw displeasure rolling inside him. He remembered Monterrey down in Nuevo Leon in Old Mexico—he'd been born there in 1850—and he remembered the scorn the grandees and those claiming noble Spanish birth had held toward his father, the freighter, and toward him, because he was an Americano, and toward his mother, whom he considered still the most gentle woman who had ever lived. Juan de Cordova had held this same scathing scorn toward him, even though this was Americano soil, but the Spanish had held this New Mexican land for centuries, and many of the so-called "gentle Spanish blood" still considered the American the intruder, not the owner. They had refused to rationalise with time.

The livery-barn hostler was a stooped old peon. He took the reins of Regan's horse, appraising the stoutness of the sorrel with one tired but practical glance.

Regan dug a bottle of Tano whiskey from a saddlebag. "You been around here long?" He tossed the bottle and gnarled hands caught it in mid-air.

He learned what he wanted to learn. The only freight outfit was the de Cordovas. Juan de Cordova had not lied —New Mexico Wagons had been owned by his family for years and years.

"Seems odd no other freighters have moved in."

Other freighters had across the century—But the de Cordovas had either bought them out, ran them out, or starved them out. Jim Regan was interested in the last explanation.

"How can a new freighter freight, when he can get no freight to haul? The de Cordovas have it all signed up on the contracts, Senor."

"Even the mines?"

"The mines they are worked and then they are not worked. Right now gold and silver are high because of the last war. In a few years it might be nothing and then the mines will close again."

Although Jim Regan had never been in Silver City before he had read all he could find about the town before leaving Deadwood in the Black Hills. These silver and gold mines were about the oldest in the United States, having been worked by Spanish slaves as far back as the sixteenth century. Pack trains consisting of thousands of mules had gone wearily south across the desert to Mexico City.

Bloody battles, political and otherwise, had been fought over these mines, and the treasures north in the high Mogollon Mountains. Redskins had finally driven

11

the Spanish south and for many years then these mines had lain idle and unworked, again awaiting the coming of the white man's pick.

Early in the eighteenth century, warring Comanches had driven Apaches from the Colorado and Texas plains, the Apaches fleeing west into the mountains and deserts, making the Mogollons and Pinos Altos their strongholds. Now the Civil War, fourteen years past, had almost bankrupt the United States, sending gold and silver prices to the heights, and Silver City, despite Apache terror, was booming again.

Watery eyes studied him. "What you do here, Senor? You are not the miner. You look the man with cows."

Regan nodded and lied, "Yes, I'm a cowman. I'm thinking of trailing in a herd from Amarillo, over in Texas. This town should use a lot of beef. But before I trail in I'll need pasture. Know where any is?"

The viejo talked slowly. For many years there had been drought. The mountains were without grass, but Jim Regan had already seen that—not enough grass to keep a goat. And two hundred hungry mules needed lots of grass.

Jim Regan waited impatiently.

"The de Cordovas have many mules and horses. All the grass we have here comes from the irrigation."

"How many irrigated areas are there?"

Two grimy old fingers rose. "Dos."

"Where are they?"

"North of town. Senor Sledge he has the dam in Silver Creek. But you cannot touch his grass."

"Why not?"

"It is leased to the de Cordovas. They graze their mules and stock there. They have had the land leased for muches chos."

Jim Regan had expected this. He wondered if he had not been foolish to make this long trek down here, burdened by bulky mules, without having scouted ahead first. But it was almost two thousand miles northeast to the Black Hills. The scouting trip, down here and back, even by rails, would have taken months, and mules would have remained idle eating their heads off in expensive hay.

"And the other irrigated section? Don't tell me the de Cordovas have that leased, too."

The wrinkled face cracked in a smile. "No, they do not lease that land." Jim Regan's heart jumped. "But it has little, if any, grass, even if the water is there from Saguaro Creek, for the Senor Enrique Williams he does not pay much attention to his land—he does not even run water on it."

"Why not?"

"He is the wild man, the lunatic, Senor Williams. Always he is back on the Gila, in the Mogollons, looking for the lost mine, the Lost Adam mine of gold."

Jim Regan knew nothing about the Lost Adam mine and right now he didn't care a whoop about it.

"Where is his outfit?"

"You go out of Silver City south, then you circle the hill called La Plata, going west, and then you come to his fence, for he has his place on Saguaro Creek, and

14

there is a fence and a gate. But the place—" Here the viejo shook his head sadly. "—has poco grass."

Jim Regan dug in his pocket and came out with a silver peso. He laid his finger across his lips, then the old man's, and the peso changed hands. The viejo nodded, smiled widely, laid his own forefinger across his cracked lips, and Jim Regan left.

Across the street, two Mexican huskies were heaving silver bars into a New Mexico Wagon's Studebaker, and Regan guessed the bars would go south-east across the desert to El Paso del Norte, commonly known only as El Paso. Two spans of mules were hitched to the Studebaker, for the silver made a heavy load, and, being a freighter, Jim gave them a careful eye, paying no attention to the leaders. A man could always hire another Mexican or Irishman, but he had to pay hard cash for a mule.

They were good mules, heavy of shoulder and rump, and Regan guessed they had come out of Old Mexico, from

15

around Chihuahua. Leather was strong and good, too, on their broad backs, well-oiled and glistening black. The wagon was also rather new, painted a bright green, with the legend NEW MEXICO WAGONS on the sideboard, painted in gaudy red.

From the open doors of cantinas and saloons came roaring laughter, the high pitch of a woman singing in Spanish, and Regan quickly noticed that the only language heard was Spanish, and he thought wryly that his Spanish had not been used for six years, the length of time he'd spent in the Hills.

He had a strong and pleasant feeling of himself, like that of a man who has lost something precious and again has found it, and he knew that was because he was again among Mexicans, hearing their lilting tongue, smelling the *frijoles fritos* —fried beans—and the thousand other smells that only Mexicans can furnish, all part of the soil, part of the people, part of their destinies. Silver City reminded him of Laredo, but here there was no stinking Rio Grande, just the sweep of desert air over clean sand and rock.

Two men came rolling out of a cantina, shouting and hammering each other in drunken fun, and one stumbled, the other falling on him in the street. They got to their feet, drunkenness changing their moods swiftly, and they fell to slugging, fighting in clean and crushing abandon. Jim Regan paid them no heed. He crossed the sagging wooden porch of the New Mexico House, entered and went to the desk. He found himself speaking Spanish.

"A room, for the night. Only I, no other."

The clerk had no rooms. The gringos from the mines—the supervisors, engineers—had every room, and had for months now. But he could furnish a bath and he summoned a heavy-set Mexican woman from the back room.

"Margo, agua caliente. Bena, para el hombre, pronto."

He led Jim Regan down a dark hall to a back room. Here was a huge wooden tub. Regan undressed and the man said,

"Your monies and other things—you keep them. I refresh your clothes."

Regan was in the tub when the Mexican woman came with two wooden buckets of warm water. She spilled them carefully into the tub, her eyes taking in his bare muscular body.

"The Americano—he wants a woman?"

Regan smiled. "Not particularmente."

She leaned over to test the water. She leaned enough to let him see her breasts, tightly bound, huge, hugging her body. He judged her to be about thirty. She had Yaqui in her, he guessed, and with Indian and Mexican, they sometimes grew heavy before their time. He judged her body to be hard and compact, good to a hungry man's grip.

Her brown eyes were but a few feet from his blue eyes. He saw round liquid eyes, bold yet frank.

"You have been a long time without a woman, no es verdad?"

Regan soaped his hairy chest. "Almost six months."

"You would like me. I am good in la cama. The others—they tell me that. You can be rough and I will respond. I charge but two pesos."

Jim Regan's heart hammered. His blood roared with hunger, and he wanted her; still, at the same time, he did not want her. He got the feeling she was soiled—she had admitted that—and while he was not so foolish to expect a virgin, there was still something about prostitution he did not like.

"I have no bed," he said.

"We can go to my house. I will chase out mio muchachos. I have the cama."

Regan patted her on the behind. "Enough of this, hermana. Wash the man's back."

She lathered him and scrubbed him. Once she leaned over and kissed him full on the mouth, her tongue making motions. Regan smiled and said no all over again, and stood up. She washed his legs and then he stepped out on the mat and she rubbed him down until his flesh glowed in health.

"Some other time, Senor?"

"Some other time," Regan assured, but he knew there would be no other time. "Where are my clothes?"

She stuck her head out the back door and hollered. Soon a barefooted lad of about fifteen entered with his clothes. He was surprised to find he had a different shirt, clean and ironed, and new underwear. His worn blue pants had been carefully brushed and his boots polished.

"My hijo," Margo said. "My oldest son."

The boy had bought the shirt and underwear at the store. Jim Regan thanked him, paid his bill, gave them each two pesos extra, and walked back into the lobby, feeling again like a member of the human race. He paid his bath bill and went outside.

The saloon across the street held the legend that *Here Billy Bonney Killed His First Man*. The mines were changing shifts and the joint was crowded, smelling of unwashed bodies, more frijoles fritos, and stale booze. Roulette wheels clicked and the chuck-a-luck dealer called in a sing-song voice.

Jim Regan squeezed up to the bar. He caught the obese bartender in an idle moment and ordered beer. It was Chihuahua beer, cool and good to the taste, and he drank it quickly, feeling its coldness hit the belly-duct. He was turning away when a burly man hit his elbow.

Regan thought, That was no accident.

He looked at the man. The man stood wide-legged staring at him. Regan saw a wide-faced American, heavy of shoulder and gut, wide of thigh. A jagged scar, evidently carved by machete or knife, was livid and red on the right jowl, running almost from the eye socket to the point of his hairy chin.

"You the guy who manhandled my boss?"

"If you refer to Juan de Cordova," Regan said quietly, "you got the guilty party."

Without warning the man flung up his heavy forearm. Regan blocked, thinking the man intended to club him across the face. But the forearm achieved its purpose, that of knocking Regan's hat to the sawdust floor.

"You use a crude approach." Jim Regan's jaw muscles were tight, standing out like small ropes. "I'll trouble you to pick up my hat."

"You pick it up."

Regan said, "I asked you to pick it up. A Mexican boy just cleaned it for me."

"Make me."

Jim Regan hit him flush on the scar. The blow drove the man back two steps. Regan had felled men with a similar overhand right.

"So you want fists, huh?"

The man came in, fists working. Regan moved swiftly to his right to make the right-fist miss. He wished he'd eaten a hearty steak upon arrival in Silver City. He'd eaten nothing since daylight camp. And this man was tough. He'd shaken off that overhand right like a duck does water.

"Get outside, you bastards!"

That dim voice belonged to the

22

bartender. Another right connected and Regan found himself against the far wall, a broken chair at his feet. He remembered vaguely tripping over the chair sending its occupant scurrying. Another right smashed into his high ribs. He came off the wall, plans made. To fight this man close would be to invite disaster. Stay away, use his left, footwork. Keep moving, darting in, darting out—use your left hand, Regan.

His mouth bled and his ribs were numb. He came in with a hook that landed flush on the big mouth, bringing blood. Another overhand right knocked the man down.

Regan spat blood and panted. "Pick up my hat."

The bartender said, "No more fighting in here, savvy?"

Regan paid him no attention. The man got on his hands and knees. He shook his head slowly, blood trickling in a line across sawdust. Then he came in, tackling Regan around the legs.

Regan went down, the man on top.

Regan took hard punishment around the face. He got his legs doubled, boots in the large gut, and kicked. He lifted the man from him. He got to his feet, and went to work again. His fists broke cartilage with a popping sound.

The man went against the wall, hovered there for a long moment, then sat down. Regan's fists had slashed a cut over his right eye. His nose was to one side, a red bulb.

He sat there, legs extended. He looked at Regan through dazed eyes.

"Pick up my hat!"

The bartender asked, "What t'hell you tryin' to prove, stranger?"

Regan kept his eyes on his opponent. "Just that I'm tougher'n he is. You getting my hat or do you want more?"

The man got on his hands and knees. He crept forward slowly toward the hat. Blood covered the front of his dirty blue shirt. His trembling big hand crept out, fingering across sawdust, and found the hat. He sat down and handed the hat to Regan.

24

"Thanks."

Regan put on the hat. His ribs were fire, blood was in his mouth, and his shirt was torn, revealing areas of red pummelled flesh.

"Who's payin' for the furniture?"

Regan looked at the bartender. "He is. He started it." The air wasn't good, foul and stinking, and he went outside. A crowd had gathered and he walked through it toward the water trough, knees weak.

Although the water was tepid, with a green grassy scum, it was somewhat cool, and he took the bucket, dipped it full of water, and poured it over his head, being careful first to remove his hat. He stood wide-legged, soaking wet, when Maria de Cordova came.

She wore a black dress that accentuated her tiny waist and flaring hips. Facets of glistening sunlight danced through her copper-colored hair.

"You seem the type that takes small things seriously," she said.

"Like picking up a hat?"

"Si, little things like that."

He mopped his face with his blue bandanna. He had a cut inside his bottom lip and he knew his left eye would be black. His ribs ached from mauling fists.

He swung his gaze toward the saloon. Two men came out supporting his opponent between them. They steered him down the street, evidently to the doctor.

"He work for you?"

"Our wagon boss. Primero."

Jim Regan folded his wet handkerchief. "What's his name?"

"Frank Morrison."

Regan looked toward New Mexico Wagons' office. Her brother sat again on the bench in the shade. His suit clean, razor-pressed, and he was immaculate. But he was something else, too—he was strong and patient and smart, and of this Regan was sure.

Juan de Cordova watched with hands folded on his lap. Regan went to him, water dripping spots in the dust.

Except for an occasional pain in his

ribs, he was himself again—resilient and jerkline tough. The saddle weariness that had been his upon riding into Silver City was gone, pushed into discard by the bath and excitement of the fight.

He stopped in front of Juan de Cordova.

"You send Morrison against me?"

Cordova's dark eyes showed nothing. His thin lips moved. "Maybe I did, and maybe I didn't."

Regan's hands became fists. "I think you did." He glanced at Maria de Cordova, who stood beside him. He expected her face to show something— fear, hatred, terror. But it did not. The lips were calm, the eyes steady. He looked back at Juan de Cordova.

"You intend to backhand me." Cordova's voice was a mere whisper. "I am not one to use fists unless forced to." He looked down at his hands. He opened his fingers daintily.

Regan saw the gun, then. A derringer, tiny and shining. The muscles along his belly tightened and his scalp crawled. Not from fear of the bullet, but from another fear—tetanus. These gambler guns could make a hole in a man. If that hole were in the right place they could kill. But his was part of the fear of many in the West, the fear of lockjaw. More than one man had died from one of these toy pistols. And not from the bullet, but from tetanus.

The long well-kept fingers flicked idly, then covered the derringer. Juan de Cordova had a flat dead voice.

"I don't know your purpose in Silver City, Senor. But I do know one thing, and that for sure."

"And that?"

Cordova's voice carried only to Regan and his sister. "Silver City is not a town for gringos. Although Silver City is geographically in the Territory of New Mexico under the gringo flag it is in actuality still a part of Mexico, a section of Spain, because we Mexicans, we Spaniards, even though of Spanish descent, control this town. We own the mines. Our people work the mines. Our

28

people are merchants and traders—the only merchants in town. We have a sheriff. You can appeal to him."

Regan's brows lifted. "An honest sheriff," he said cynically.

Cordova sighed. "Yes, he is honest—when we of Spanish blood are involved, when we who run this town are concerned. But to gringos—" He left the sentence unfinished.

Regan noticed he had not used the word Americano, only gringo. And gringo, coming from such lips, was an insult—you might just as well call a man a son-of-a-bitch.

Regan held his temper, remembering that derringer.

"So you will get on your horse, now, and leave, gringo? I think it is the best thing, no?"

"No."

Regan turned and left.

2

HE bought a new shirt in a store. He changed to it in the storeroom in the back, wadding up the shirt Margo's boy had delivered, thinking ironically that he had not worn the shirt an hour. Then he went to a cafe. The dinner rush was not on yet and he had an empty stool on each side. Soon he was aware of a man sliding onto the stool at his right.

"What'll it be, sheriff?" the waitress asked.

"Coffee." Tersely.

From the corner of one eye Jim Regan saw a dark-skinned man with a heavy-jowled face, greying hair, meaty shoulders and a belly slightly too big. The coffee came and Regan saw blunt fingers cradle the cup.

"You the fellow that had the fight with Frank Morrison?"

Regan looked into small dark eyes. The trouble with Mexicans was that their eyes seldom showed anything, being so damn' dark.

He nodded.

"Your name?"

The man had a deep throaty voice. Regan wondered if he did not have bronchial trouble. The voice seemed to start out okay, then flatten out to a hoarse whisper. It was the type of voice a man would forever remember once he heard it.

"Jim Regan."

"Where from?"

"My business."

The cup rose steadily. Its rim found heavy lips. Regan saw nothing in the olive-skinned face.

"Your business in Silver City?"

"Also my business. And mine alone."

The cup came down. It touched the counter without a sound. The sheriff's lips moved a little, then became still again.

"You make this hard for me," that throaty voice said. "Morrison may die, you know. Doc thinks maybe he got a fractured skull when his head hit the wall. Doc took fourteen stitches in that rip in Morrison's hide." Heavy fingers turned the coffee cup slowly. "Lay your hands on the table?"

"You arresting me?"

"No . . . not yet."

Regan put his hands palm-down on the table.

"Thought maybe you wore a big ring. You must hit hard as a mule kicks to slice that cut without a ring." The cup rose again. "I'd still like to know your business here."

Regan thought, Sure if I told you you'd head hell-for-leather and tell your bosom pals, the de Cordovas, and right off I'd lose what little chance I have of getting Senor Williams' grass.

"Riding through, that's all."

The black eyes sparkled. "Well, then keep on riding."

Regan's steak came. He cut into it and it was like butter. "You're sort of wasting your time—and mine, Sheriff." He told

32

about the three wagons and the Apaches.

"Juan de Cordova told me about them. I sent a man out to check. I also got word to Fort Bayard. I doubt if the cavalry will have time for such a small thing, though."

"Small thing? Three drivers were murdered and thrown into the fire. Six head of mules were butchered and toted off on pack horses."

The sheriff put centavos on the table and got to his feet. "Victorio jumped his reservation a few months ago over on the Mescalero. He's got these Mimbres Apaches stirred up. Night before last they sacked the Tres Pinos ranch back on the Gila about fifty miles."

Sweat popped out on Jim Regan's thighs. He remembered what he'd seen— the rifles puffing smoke, the lift and fall of the war-axe, the sharp canine yaps of blood-thirsty redskin killers.

"They burned the big outfit to the ground. Everything and everybody went —the entire Guadalupe family—all the vaqueros that happened to be on the home ranch—Did you ever see a mutilated scalped little girl?"

"Yes."

"Where?"

"Sioux."

"Then you know now why three burned wagons and three dead drivers are not so damned important."

"What's wrong with the cavalry?"

"Nothing. Only there's mighty few of them stationed. Crook held the Apaches down—he's a good hand with redskins—but five months ago the army moguls sent General Crook up to Colorado, because the redskins were acting up up there."

Regan nodded. Well did he know of the Ute rebellion. He and Old Wad and the Mexican had had to swing their mules east, driving almost to the Kansas line, to escape the trouble.

"When will Crook be back?"

Heavy shoulders shrugged. "God knows, I guess. These army moguls sit behind big desks in Washington. They move generals and troops around to suit their own fancy, not the wishes and wants of those who need troops the most out here in the desert. There's talk about sending General Nelson A. Miles south. There's even talk that Fort Bayard is going to be shut down. With it gone, we'll have no protection but our rifles and knives and hand-guns."

"Apaches ever hit de Cordova freight?"

The sheriff stood up. "Not as yet."

"Seems odd they'd jump on those three wagons. They were empty."

"They wanted the mules for grub. Apaches like nothing better than a haunch of roasted mule. Another thing is that the de Cordovas freight south across the desert. Apaches like to raid in the rough country. Also Fort Bayard sends troops with each de Cordova wagon train and stage. You seem awful interested in the de Cordovas."

"Maria de Cordova is a beauty."

The sheriff regarded him for a moment. "You can fall outa line there, Buster. She's got her pick of about ten millionaires. One mine owner's son would give his back teeth to latch onto her."

"Lucky stiff."

To the onlooker it would appear that the sheriff and Jim Regan were merely passing the time of the day, but Regan knew otherwise. This man, although too fat for his height, was tough underneath, and what he wanted he would get by brains and stealth and politics, not by gun or brawn. But in the last resort, if brains and the others failed, he would use his gun, and of this Regan was sure. He could smell it. He could taste this. He could feel it. This conversation, apparently rambling, was in actuality a warning —get out of my town and stay out because you can't buck us Mexicans and our power and wealth, whoever and whatever you are.

The sheriff said, "So long," and left.

Regan did not look at him; he regarded what was left of his steak. He finished his meal in thoughtful silence, paid the Mexican waitress, and left, going to the barn. Dusk had come quickly, a habit of this high country at this time of the year, and the northern mountains, the Pinos Altos, were dark now, unseen against time and distance.

He felt sure now that the burned freight-wagons were wagons he'd ordered. His sale agreement with Ramosa in El Paso had guaranteed delivery of the wagons to Silver City.

He had ordered the wagons made last April, sending Ramosa a money-order of five hundred bucks as a retainer. That had been a month before William Hearst's own Black Hills railroad had pulled its first freight into Deadwood. His mind flicked back to that day in his Deadwood office.

"This railroad will take our place. We're through here, Wad."

Old Wad Emerson cursed as only an ancient muleskinner can curse. "Just like in Laredo, Texas. The revolution drove us out of Monterrey in Mexico. We left your father there killed. Eighteen sixty four, and it seems like a thousand years ago."

Jim Regan toyed with a pencil, sitting in his swivel chair in front of his desk, gazing unseeingly out at the mountainside, now turning green under spring rains and spring sun.

"Then Laredo, Texas. Freighting between there and San Antone. We were driven out by rails there, too. We left your mother there. Now these damn' rails are putting us out of business again."

Jim Regan nodded in silence.

Old Wad tugged his grey beard. Short, wiry, tough as jerked buffalo, five-foot-six, one hundred and ten pounds dripping wet, almost seventy.

"So we have to move again. Now where t'hell you going to leave Wad Emerson?"

"You'll live forever."

"Where do we go, Jim?"

"Silver City."

"Territory of New Mexico. Never been there. Have you?"

"No. I've talked to miners here who've just come from Silver City. The mines are booming there."

"Any railroads?"

38

"None into Silver City. Santa Fe is going down the Rio Grande but that's a hundred miles east. Southern Pacific is laying rails through Lordsburg sixty miles south."

"Where do they freight to?"

"El Paso, about a hundred and fifty miles south-east. El Paso is the end of rails west. Freight comes up out of Chihuahua, Old Mexico, too."

Now Jim Regan had sour thoughts. Freighting would be a hard nut to crack here. Maybe he couldn't crack it? And those burned wagons—

Ramosa's skinners had missed the Espejo Trail. They'd swung too far north. They'd travelled the Mimbres Trail.

The de Cordovas had all contracts. Well, a contract was only made to be broken.

Two hundred gaunt, belly-flat mules. Mules that needed good pasture to put on hard flesh. No pasture, he couldn't stay in Silver City.

He needed more than pasture: barns, a bunkhouse, messhall, sleeping quarters, a

39

cook, an oiler. Yes and harnesses and wagons.

And he needed freight to haul.

You had to keep mules on the move. You had to have filled wagons, busy crews. You had to hustle. You had to have a paying load going out, another coming in. Never empty wagons.

First you had to have pasture.

He left his horse in the barn. They would be watching his horse—the sheriff, the de Cordovas. He ducked down an alley, skirted some adobe buildings, and was on the south outskirts of Silver City.

He remembered the old hostlers words. First, circle the toe of the hill called La Plata. The Silver. Then you come to Saguaro Creek and a gate. North of there is Senor Enrique Williams' land.

Behind him on the hill kerosene lamps glowed in mine offices. Gradually the pound of machinery moved back. La Plata Hill would be the hill on the west side of town. Here ran a wagon trail apparently little used. He followed it through high manzanita and chamisal.

Within a mile he came to a rock fence as high as a man. It ran about a half-mile between two hills. Behind it was a broad valley to the north.

Regan found a wooden gate. A chain and a padlock. He climbed the gate, pausing for a moment, listening. He heard nothing but the soughing of wind in red-shank. Through the dim moonlight he saw a set of buildings up ahead hugging the west flank of a hill.

They had no lights.

That would be Senor Williams' buildings. The dim wagon trail led toward them but he did not follow it. He strode out into the fields. He heard dry grass rustle under his boots. He went to one knee, felt, got a handful of grass, tasted it. Alfalfa. Dry. Needing water. He dug down. But alfalfa, with good roots. Once it had water it would rear up out of the desert soil.

He stood up and looked around.

He judged the area to be about two hundred acres. La Plata Hill lay on the east and another high hill on the west.

North about a mile the two hills met, making an arrowhead shaped valley.

Where was Saguaro Creek? He heard no running water.

Moonlight was very dim. He fell suddenly, and found himself in a small arroyo, plainly a creek bed but now dry with thick sand. He got to his feet and walked along it. A quarter-mile from the north end of the spread his boots became wet and he sank into sand. He scrambled out, boots muddy, knowing all there was to know about Saguaro Creek.

The creek came through the narrow north defile. Then it hit the sand and disappeared, a habit with these desert-mountain creeks.

He found the dam. It was made of rock and concrete, about two hundred feet long, impounding water back into the gorge—quite a lake of water, he saw. The west end had a concrete spillway. Water ran over the concrete apron about an inch deep to lose itself in Saguaro Creek.

The main turn-out gate, made of steel, was in good shape, although padlocked down. All a man had to do was open it and water would run into the main canal. Then onto alfalfa fields.

And alfalfa would grow quickly.

This was just what he needed in pasture. He went to the buildings. The main building was of adobe—a long dark streak under moonlight. There was a barn, a blacksmith shop, a long frame messhall. All buildings were locked. He could see little through dirty windows.

This had been a Spanish hacienda. Some of these buildings were almost two hundred years old. Once this had been a big rancho, sufficient to itself—a town by itself.

Nothing moved. He was the only living thing on this rancho. No horses, no cattle, no ducks, chickens, no dogs. No humans. Or was there a human? He flattened against a wall listening, eyes peering.

He'd heard a boot hit something.

Senor Enrique Williams?

No, not if the hostler were correct. Senor Williams was out chasing a will-of-the-wisp, the Lost Adam mine. But the hostler could be wrong.

Jim Regan crouched in the L made by the house's porch. Here moonlight did not penetrate.

He listened. A weird feeling gripped him, tugging at his blood. He waited. Time ran on silently. He thought, just the wind, banging something somewhere. Then he heard it again.

The man came slowly. He was dark, big. He walked on catfeet. Moonlight drifted in, momentarily showing his huge face. Jim saw the jagged scar. The man paused, close to the adobe, back to Jim Regan.

Regan came in. His gun-barrel lifted, fell. The man fell, too—his knees bent, he went down on his face.

Regan stood over him, rubbing his gun barrel on his leg. The sheriff had lied. Morrison was not in bed with a fractured skull.

Morrison lay here on the ground.

3

EARLY dawn covered the mountainous desert. Ghost trees, down in dry washes, stood out grey, eerie. Jim Regan's pistol bucked three times. The third bullet opened the padlock.

Old Wad Emerson rode in and swung open the heavy gate. Jim Regan stood on stirrups and waved to the Mexican who suddenly came to life hightailing the mules ahead onto Williams' grass.

They thundered in, long-eared, mean, ugly. They smelled water and feed and they needed water and grass. The last loped through, dust-grimed and bony, and the Mexican pulled in his tired horse, grinning widely.

"Well," he said, "we made it, hombres."

His name was Pedro. He was fat, squat, oily, with a wide nose and thick lips, and

Jim had met him in Denver, hired him, and here they were—mules grazing on dried short alfalfa that was dying for water.

"What about this bucko?" Old Wad jerked a thumb toward Frank Morrison. Morrison rode slouched in saddle, hands tied to the horn. This was the beginning of the fourth day Morrison had been tied to his horse.

"I'll deliver him to his mama and papa," Jim Regan said.

"Want me to go along?" Old Wad asked.

Jim shook his head. "You and Pedro stay with the mules. Haze them up toward water. The dam's up that way." He pointed north with his chin.

Pedro glanced anxiously at the Williams buildings. "What if the Senor Williams is home?"

"You boys take care of that," Jim Regan said.

Old Wad scratched his bald head. He had only a wide fringe of hair left and this gave his seamed bearded face a comic look.

"Mules on grass we haven't leased. No freight contracts. Short feed, no hands, damn' little money."

"Anything else?" Jim asked.

Old Wad smiled suddenly. "Good luck." He and Pedro started slowly hazing the mules north. Jim turned toward Silver City leading the horse carrying Frank Morrison.

Morrison croaked, "Why not turn me loose, Regan? I'll pull out, honest to God. I'll drift south to Lordsburg. You'll never see me again."

"You afraid of the de Cordovas?"

"No."

"I agree with you, Morrison. Juan de Cordova has a little sting-gun, though. One night over in Dodge I saw a gambler shoot a trailhand with a derringer. The bullet made only a small hole in the cowpuncher's arm."

"Yeah?"

"But that cowhand died in five days or so. You know, lockjaw set in that wound

47

—and docs can't do a thing about it. A man's throat gets tight, he wants to drink, burns with thirst, but can't swallow a drop."

"You don' say."

"So he dies."

"Juan de Cordova ain't shot me yet, Regan."

"You got that big Navy .44 and Maria de Cordova—ah, there's a beauty for you, clean, wholesome. You work for the de Cordova's. Maria might even kiss you seeing she's so glad you're back."

"You ain't funny."

By the time they reached the office of New Mexico Wagons quite a crowd of miners, Mexicans, children and dogs accompanied them. Juan de Cordova again sat on the bench in the shade.

Jim Regan drew rein, halting Morrison's horse also.

He watched Juan de Cordova's eyes.

Black, shiny, they were moving marbles in the gaunt, well-shaven face. They seared Morrison with hard fire, then switched to Jim Regan.

"I brought your man back," Jim Regan said.

Juan de Cordova merely nodded. Regan wondered if he were not so mad he did not trust words.

"He trailed me out of town three nights ago," Jim Regan said. "We had a little meeting out in the brush. Since then he likes me so well he won't leave me. But shucks, I ain't got any use for him."

All the time he was untying Morrison's hands. This done he gave Morrison a tough push that spilled the man into the dust.

"He'll have a story to tell you," Jim Regan said. He looked for a moment at Morrison who was climbing out of the dust on weak knees. When he looked up again Maria de Cordova stood in the office door. She had a pencil in her hand.

Jim Regan smiled. "Hello, Maria."

Her eyes became cloudy. Her lips opened, then came shut quickly. She looked at Morrison and then at her brother. "What is the matter?"

She ignored Jim Regan.

Well, you won't ignore me long, Regan thought. By God, I'll bend you to your knees—if it's fight you want, this gringo can supply it.

"Morrison will tell you all about it." Regan rode away. He stopped in front of the bank. Standing on the steps of the bank he looked back. The de Cordovas and Morrison were gone and the crowd was breaking up.

The banker stood looking out the window. He'd watched Regan take Morrison to town. He turned. Regan saw a typical Mexican banker. Pot belly, full face, blue serge suit with worn cuffs.

"What's the disturbance?"

Regan walked through the swinging gate. He sat in the banker's chair behind the banker's desk. A clerk glanced up from his ledgers in surprise. And the banker frowned angrily.

"You're taking a lot on yourself," the banker said.

Regan dug out his knife. He took off his right boot and opened the top stitching and dumped the boot upside down. Greenbacks fluttered to the floor. The book-keeper forgot his ledger.

The banker forgot his anger.

The banker smiled widely. He stooped laboriously, bending his gut, to pick up the money. Regan brought his right foot down hard on the plump wrist, imprisoning it.

The banker stared up at him, eyes bulging in sockets.

"Keep your hands to yourself," Regan advised.

Regan pulled his foot back. The banker straightened, rubbing his wrist. Regan picked up the hundred dollar notes. He counted them. Forty nine.

He dug into his boot and came up with one more. He stacked them in a pile on the banker's desk.

"Five thousand dollars oro," he said.

He kicked off his left boot, split it, and came up with fifty more one hundred dollar bills. He handed the boots to the book-keeper.

"Take these to the bootmaker. Get

them sewed up and do it pronto." It was not a request; it was an order.

The book-keeper glanced at the banker who nodded red-faced. The book-keeper picked up the boots and left.

The banker extended a plump hand. "Senor Jaime Lamas."

"Put that money in a checking account."

The banker counted the bills slowly, wetting a flat thumb. "Ten thousand dollars oro even."

The banker went to a counter and made out a deposit book. Once he glanced at Regan sitting in his, the banker's, chair. The banker wanted that chair to work in, but he said nothing. He dug under the counter and got a check book.

Regan said, "I'll also need a letter of verification."

The banker raised inquisitive brows.

"El Paso," Regan said shortly. "Buying wagons and harness there. Nobody there knows my checks."

The banker got pen and paper and started to scratch. Regan extended his legs and looked at his feet. The book-keeper returned with his boots. "Fast job," Regan said, and pulled on the boots.

The banker finally finished the letter. Regan read it and folded it and put it in his wallet.

The banker cleared his throat. "You intend to go into business in Silver City, Senor Regan?"

"Freighting."

"Oh, freighting." The banker nodded. "The de Cordovas have had all freight in and out of Silver City for years and years. Do you have mules and wagons and harnesses and—"

"That's my business."

"You sound rather—well, unfriendly."

"I am unfriendly."

Regan looked at the ten thousand now encased by a wide rubber band. His life-time savings. Years of howling Dakota-Wyoming blizzards, of scorching Texas sun, of mosquitoes, bulky mules, bulky skinners, broken-down axles, broken traces. Ten thousand lousy bucks and two hundred gaunt mules.

And the last freighting town.

"The minute I'm out of here," Jim Regan said, "either you or one of your hands will scoot over to Juan de Cordova's office. You'll give him a blow by blow story."

"You evidently don't like bankers?"

"Parasites. Sometimes necessary parasites, though. The only reason I'm depositing this money is because I don't want to get robbed by thugs."

"You'll find freighting—"

"I know all about it. The de Cordovas have all freighting under contract. Have had for years and years."

He went out into the sunlight. He had a cold clammy feeling. The bank had tasted, smelled, looked like a tomb. He saw the sheriff crossing the street. He waited on the plank sidewalk.

"I thought you left town."

"I did. I came back. I'm here in the flesh. Something you want? You know, we've had a nice friendly talk, but you never did give me your name."

"Lucas Garcia, Sheriff of this county."

"I know you're sheriff. You warned me to leave town, remember. What're you doing about those burned freight wagons, those three dead freighters, those six stolen mules?"

"The army is trailing those Apaches. A cavalry detachment is back in the Pinos Altos now."

"Probably commanded by a bunch of braid that couldn't find its way around Fort Bayard's barracks."

"Why you so interested in those wagons?"

"They were my wagons. Sent out by Ramosa, from El Paso. I dug in the ashes. I found Ramosa's nameplate there."

"You—a freighter?"

The sheriff glanced toward the office and compound of New Mexico Wagons.

"Two hundred head of mules," Jim Regan said. "Moved them in this morning on grass I leased. The Williams ranch." He jabbed a thumb over his shoulder toward the bank. "I just deposited ten thousand oro in there. I'll tell you now to save that fat banker the trouble."

"What'll you freight?"

Jim Regan didn't answer that. He stepped forward and before the sheriff could move back his bulk Regan had ripped the badge from his shirt. It came away with a sibilant rip of cloth.

Regan threw the badge into the street dust. "Polish it with dust before you pick it up, Garcia. It needs a polish job."

Heavy jowls grew scarlet red. Tobacco-stained teeth ground savagely. Gleeful eyes watched. Regan got the impression that the watching eyes caused Sheriff Lucas Garcia's greatest humiliation. From what he'd heard, this man had been sheriff for years.

"I could jail you for this."

"You could," Regan agreed, and added, "but you won't."

Garcia bent and picked up his badge. He presented a wide and inviting rear and Jim Regan held back desire successfully. Regan walked to the corner. Sheriff Lucas

Garcia was going toward New Mexico Wagons.

Garcia entered de Cordova's office.

Jack Morrison sat on a chair. He looked the worse for wear. Maria de Cordova sat behind her desk. Juan de Cordova leaned against the wall.

The sheriff wheezed, "What t'hell's the matter?"

Maria was silent. Juan de Cordova smiled. Morrison leaned back in his chair and said nothing.

"That damned gringo Regan. You saw what he did out there, didn't you?" Sheriff Lucas Garcia did not wait for an answer.

"How come Regan take you into town tied to your horse, Morrison?"

"Ask Juan," Morrison said dryly.

"Damn it to hell, I want to know!" Anger rimmed Garcia's words.

Just then Banker Lamas came in by the back door. "This fellow Regan just deposited ten thousand in the bank. Had it sewed in his boots. Sat there big as life in my chair behind my desk ordering me around. He's going to get wagons and harnesses out of El Paso."

Juan de Cordova nodded.

Lamas said, "They tell me he's got a bunch of mules out on Enrique Williams' place."

Morrison said, "Trailed them in a while ago. Good mules, too." He grinned quietly. "I should know. I helped haze them from beyond Dos Cabezas."

"Did he lease Williams' place?" the banker asked.

"So that's the deal," Sheriff Lucas Garcia said. "Well, you got everything under contract, ain't you, Juan?"

Juan de Cordova nodded. "He never leased Williams' place," he said. "Williams is somewhere back in the Mogollons, crazy as a turpentined bat. They'd have to show me that lease before I'd believe it."

Sheriff Lucas Garcia breathed shrilly with asthmatic sharpness. Maria de Cordova looked at her pencil. Her fingers trembled slightly. She thought of Jim

Regan, holding him complete against the screen of her memory.

Tall . . . tough . . . good looking . . . She felt her skin grow moist. She compared him with the others, the ones who wanted her, and they fell short. These men—her brother, the sheriff, the banker—they thought and talked only in terms of violence. But a woman had a way. Especially a beautiful woman . . . Her brother's harsh voice brought her back.

"All right, get out, Morrison. Lucas, float Morrison out of town, if he hasn't got sense enough to leave."

Morrison got to his feet, fists doubled. "Try to run me out, you Mexican son-of-a-bitch! That goes for you, too, you potbellied bastard of a sheriff!"

Juan de Cordova started forward. Sheriff Lucas Garcia moved his bulk between the two men.

"Damn it to hell, Juan," he wheezed. "This muleskinner don't mean anything. Save your hell for Jim Regan."

"Sit down, Juan." Maria de Cordova spoke crisply.

Morrison leered. "I got some money coming."

Juan de Cordova stepped back. "Figure out his check, Maria." There was silence while Maria consulted the books. She wrote the check and handed it to Morrison who folded it without looking at it and got his hat and left. But he had one parting sentence.

"You big boys feel yourselves slipping?"

Then he was gone. Juan de Cordova walked to a chair and sat down. Banker Lamas stood in respectful silence. The sheriff kept on wheezing.

Finally Juan de Cordova asked, "Where's Judge Gonzales?"

The sheriff said, "At home, I guess. Why?"

"I know a little about law," Juan de Cordova said. He examined the sharp point of a pencil. "A crazy man's signature is no good."

The banker nodded.

"Victorio lets Williams tramp all over the Mogollons because Apacheria thinks Williams is crazy. Apaches won't touch a loco man, saying he lives in the shadow zone between life and death."

Maria de Cordova watched her brother. She saw the set of his jaw, the lines around his mouth. She remembered how Jim Regan had grabbed her brother, lifting him to his feet, and the town had watched. She remembered the tough lines of Regan's face, the harshness of his eyes. And suddenly she felt dreadfully cold.

"Send for Judge Gonzales," Juan de Cordova said. "I want to talk to the judge."

4

REGAN sat across the desk from Matthew Valenzuela, owner of El Marcado, Silver City's biggest general store. Through the closed door came the hum of customers.

"I'm perfectly satisfied with New Mexico Wagons, Mr. Regan. I've run this establishment for thirty-four years last June. All these years New Mexico Wagons have done my freighting. Before Juan de Cordova and his sister took over the freighting business, their father ran it."

"And before their father, their grandfather."

Valenzuela glanced at him sharply, then smiled. "I guess you've heard that from everybody you've talked to today."

Regan nodded. "From the mines. The saloons. The other stores." He got to his feet, hiding his weariness. "What do you pay them per pound per mile to move freight?"

Valenzuela's gaunt eyes fell to his desk. "I hardly think the terms of our contract with New Mexico Wagons should be revealed, Mr. Regan. My contract still has six years to go, I believe. And when it expires I suppose New Mexico Wagons will still be in business for a renewal."

Jim Regan stood straight and thoughtful and black despair ran through him, turning his sinews hard and tough and stringy.

"Other freighters have tried to break the hold of New Mexico Wagons. None have done it across the years. When there is no freight to be hauled in or out of Silver City—" Valenzuela left his sentence unfinished.

"I understand New Mexico Wagons only freight south to El Paso? They don't go north to the Mogollon settlements?"

"Only a fool would try to freight in Apacheria. Apaches don't like to hit on the desert—too much open country. Cavalry from Fort Bayard accompanies

New Mexico Wagons freight-wagons and coaches."

So Fort Bayard's rifles protect New Mexico Wagons? They should also protect his wagons, then. Or did the political pull of the de Cordovas go even into the military?

"Any towns in the Mogollon?" Regan asked.

"The town of Mogollon is the biggest, about a hundred. Prospectors and miners work out from there. It's on the San Francisco river, north of the Gila river—about ninety miles northwest." Valenzuela's eyes narrowed. "To get there you go right through Victorio's backyard. You aren't thinking of freighting through Apacheria, for God's sake?"

"Where does Mogollon get its supplies?"

"There's only one general store in town. The owner freights out of here—I sell him wholesale. But there hasn't been a man in from Mogollon for three weeks. From what they tell me the town is a fortress—nobody going in, nobody going out. Only one man moves back and forth and that's Enrique Williams. Apaches think he is crazy and they won't touch a demented man."

Regan nodded, and left.

He went to the post office. The day was sinking—he's spent it talking to mine superintendents, merchants, tradesmen.

He had one letter. Ramosa, the wagon-maker, down in El Paso. Ramosa was sending three wagons north. The others would be delivered within two weeks from the first shipment.

Regan toyed with the letter and thought, word will get back to him about three burned wagons, three dead skinners, six slaughtered mules. Ramosa would not attempt to deliver the others. Within a few days a letter would come telling him, Jim Regan, to come after the wagons, if he wanted them.

Regan went to the newspaper office. It was a weekly, printed in Spanish, and the editor was named Joseph Cortinas.

They dickered and Jim Regan bought half a page for one hundred dollars.

Cortinas showed him a desk and gave him some paper. The sheet would come out tomorrow—already presses somewhere back in the cool adobe building were grinding out the paper's centre sections. Regan had composed quite a few ads in his business, but this was the most difficult he'd been called on to write.

"You got a cut of a freight wagon and mules?"

"The one I used to use for New Mexico Wagons. They don't advertise but just once in a while. When you get all the business under lock and key you don't have to buy space."

His tone was resentful.

Regan looked up. "Apparently you don't like the de Cordovas too much?" A shot in the dark. Somewhere there had to be a slit in this town's monetary armour.

Cortinas looked at his ink-dark fingers. Regan judged him to be about forty, but he was not heavy like most Mexicans— he was flat-bellied and without excess weight.

"Look, Senor Regan, get something

straight. I print and sell a newspaper. To keep my newspaper running in the black I have to sell advertising. You've raised a lot of hell in this town. You insulted Sheriff Garcia before the whole town. Garcia might be fat but he's proud. You called Juan de Cordova's hand. You shook him like a terrier shaking a rat. Don't sell Juan de Cordova short— he's smart, wealthy, and he can be dangerous."

Regan nodded, eyes on the man.

"You whipped hell out of Frank Morrison, *primero* for New Mexico Wagons. You took Morrison on a trip with you, tied to his saddle. You know, you'll take up quite a bit of space on my front page."

"Free advertising."

"Maybe so. But I have to ride the middle line."

"For money?"

"Yes, for that filthy thing called *dinero*."

"I see your point. That's why I freight. That's why I'm buying space for this ad.

But there's something in your voice that tells me you're unhappy about Silver City, *Senor* Cortinas."

"You imagine things, *Senor* Regan. I own a nice home. I have a wonderful wife and seven children. I own this building; everything in it is clear of debt. But don't forget that Juan de Cordova is a powerful man. His father was mayor for years. I have to travel with the controlling class. I really shouldn't take your ad."

Regan spoke with cynicism "I feel sorry for you."

He finshed the ad and handed it to Cortinas who showed him a proof of the cut showing a freight wagon. Cortinas slowly read the ad.

"You offer to cut New Mexico Wagons' freight rate by ten per cent. You offer faster service. You'll haul mail free for six months." Cortinas smiled. "You can't break a government contract, you know."

"I know that. But it sounds good on paper." Regan got to his feet with his muscles, his sinews, demanding action.

"Who hauls government freight to Fort Bayard?"

"New Mexico Wagons. I think de Cordova has a contract."

"I've freighted around dozens of army posts, and I've never heard yet of one giving a freight contract to a private company. Most of them have to haul their own freight."

"You might have found a loophole."

Regan smiled. "Maybe . . . Maybe not . . ."

"You sound mysterious."

Regan kept his voice level. "I roughed the sheriff up a little. I put some money in the bank. Right off the sheriff peglegs it to de Cordova's office. And right off I see the banker sneaking down the alley. Right now de Cordova knows to the cent what I have in that bank."

"You think I'd hightail for New Mexico Wagons, eh?"

Cortinas' face was pale. His dark eyes stood out angrily. His hands had become white-knuckled fists.

"You're one of them."

69

"Maybe I won't print this ad?"

Regan grabbed the man's shirt front in both hands. Cortinas hit at him but Regan shoved him hard. Cortinas' blow was spent on empty air. Cortinas hit a desk, moved it with his force, and steadied.

Regan watched the newspaper man's eyes. Anger left them and logic came in, blunting their sharp ugliness.

Cortinas spoke slowly. "You know, you might be the medicine Silver City needs. I'll run the ad."

"Gracias." Regan spoke dryly.

He went outside, muscles across the chest tight, pulling in clean mountain air, feeling it touch the pockets of his lungs. The muscle along his jaw stopped trembling. He looked at New Mexico Wagons.

Juan de Cordova sat in the shade in front of his office. He was talking with a heavy set elderly man who wore a brown suit and tie despite the heat. The man looked to be one of influence. He and de Cordova sat close together, and Regan noticed de Cordova did most of the talking.

De Cordova did not see him. Or, if he did, he acted otherwise. Regan went to his horse at the hitchrack.

"Regan!"

The voice came from a saloon doorway. Regan dropped his boot from stirrup. He turned quickly.

Frank Morrison stepped out of the doorway. "Didn't mean to scare you," he said, "but I wanted to talk to you before you left town."

Morrison came toward him. Regan read no menace in his advance. He looked at the swollen nose, the puffed lips, the cut over Morrison's eye, now scabbed over. His fists had done those things.

"What's on your mind?"

"I want a job."

Regan felt surprise. "I thought you were the boss for New Mexico Wagons?"

"No more." Frank Morrison spoke rather loudly. Regan realised he wanted his voice to reach Juan de Cordova. "That bastard over there on the bench just canned me."

"And now you want to work for me?"

71

"Yes."

"Why?"

"Hell, Regan, I'm a skinner, first, last always. All my life I've been around freight, mules, horses, blacksmiths, jerklines. I could go to work in the mines —prob'ly make more money. But I don't like those dark holes. Time'll come when I kick the bucket and then I'll have time for the pits."

Juan de Cordova was watching. The well-dressed elderly man sitting beside de Cordova watched, too.

"We've had trouble," Regan reminded.

"I know that. Hell, I'm not one to pack a grudge, man. You're a better man than I am. That's why I crave to get on your payroll."

Despite his battered lips, Frank Morrison wore a smile. Regan remembered the man's toughness on the long ride tied to his saddle-horn. How he never bellyached, threatened. He'd taken the ride, bumpy and miserable, in his stride. Of course, he had followed him that night out to the Williams ranch—but Regan

72

could not prove Morrison had followed to kill.

There was something else, too. This man had an air of reliability, of rough precision—when you set him to do a job, whether to shoe a mule or put a freight train through Indian danger, Regan was sure he would do it, or die in the attempt. He grudgingly admitted that he had grown to like this man somewhat.

"Where's you horse?"

Morrison said, "Tied over yonder."

"Get him."

Regan mounted and rode north. Within a quarter-mile Frank Morrison had caught him. Regan said, "Maybe you're still working for New Mexico Wagons?"

Frank Morrison quickly caught the implication. "If you'll crawl off that horse, Regan, I'll take another whack at you, and with pleasure."

Regan smiled. "What am I going to pay you with?"

"Ten thousand bucks."

Regan said, "Whenever a man puts

money in a bank nobody is supposed to tell how much his checking account is."

"This," said Frank Morrison, "is Silver City, Territory of New Mexico. And hell, that fat banker didn't tell Juan de Cordova nothing. All Juan would have had to do to find out, is look at the bank's books. He's a big stockholder in the bank, you know. Some claim he even owns one of the biggest red-light houses in town. Course, that doesn't keep him out of church each Sunday."

"Can he handle a gun?"

"He can . . . when forced. But he'd rather use his brains, or somebody else's fists or gun. I ramrodded for him for four years. I've seen him kill two men. One was a man who started another freight line. De Cordova shot him down before he could get rolling."

Regan's jaw quivered.

"Don't sell him short, Regan. He looks calm back of that handsome dark face. But he's got brains. And he's cold as a frozen catfish. Besides, he's got political pull."

74

Regan nodded.

"You seen that fellow sitting beside him? Well, that's the district judge, Alberto Gonzales. He's also a stockholder in Lamas' bank. Gonzales and Juan's old father were bosom friends. They weren't just sitting there passing the time of the day. We going to Fort Bayard?"

"That's right."

"You might be taking the right step, Regan. New Mexico Wagons doesn't hold a gover'ment contract with Fort Bayard."

"But they do haul in government supplies?"

"Yes. I got a hunch that de Cordova cuts back a nice sum to the general at Fort Bayard. Of course, I can't prove that. But I got a hunch that if you offer Hamilton more'n de Cordova does in cutback, you might get some freight to move into Bayard."

The old army game, Regan thought dryly.

Fort Bayard was about six miles northeast of Silver City. The cavalry post was situated on a wide mesa. There was no stockade made of stone or logs. The frame buildings were sun-warped and many needed paint. Only the officers' quarters had been painted recently.

The scene was one of organised hurried activity. Highwheeled freight wagons stood in front of barracks and offices. Regan glanced first at the wagons, noticing they were army issue. His second glance went to the mules. They were not much. Once again a mule trader had skinned Uncle.

Enlisted men moved furniture and personal goods out of barracks. The only people not working were six Apaches, each naked to the waist, wearing only moccasins and pants. Black braids hung over dark shoulders.

"Scouts," Morrison murmured.

Regan shook his head. "Can't understand them. They scout out and bring in army rifles to kill their own relatives and people."

"Dinero."

"Something is sure going on," Regan said.

Morrison led him directly to General Hamilton's office. The general and an aide were cleaning out a desk and the beefy commandante looked up red faced from exertion.

"Something you two want?"

Although his rough tone rankled Regan, the freighter overlooked it. He had heard that tone many times before. "I wear stars. You don't. I'm from West Point. You probably don't even know where West Point is. You're a civilian, a nuisance."

Regan introduced himself. "Those were my three wagons Victorio burned."

"I sent out a patrol. It came back about an hour ago. It found nothing." General Hamilton's fat face glistened with sweat. "Anything else, Mr. Regan?"

"I'm a freighter. I intend to freight to Mogollon."

The aide straightened suddenly. General Hamilton laid heavy eyes against Jim Regan.

"Yes, Mr. Regan."

"I understand you escort de Cordova

wagons. I would like army troops to see my wagons through to Mogollon."

General Hamilton tapped a paper on his desk. "Those wagons you see outside came in thirty minutes ago from Fort Bowie. Their Commander brought me this from Washington, DC."

Regan nodded. Morrison stood silently.

"These orders say that, on their receipt, I am to move everything—men, equipment, headquarters—to Fort Bowie. Fort Bowie is about a hundred miles from here southwest in Arizona Territory."

"You're abandoning Fort Bayard?" Regan asked. General Hamilton nodded shortly.

5

OLD Wad met them at the gate.
"We got company, boss."
"Male or female?"

"I guess you could call him male. Senor Enrique Williams, our landlord."

Regan and Morrison rode through. Jim Regan noticed Old Wad glancing inquiringly at Frank Morrison. Old Wad swung the gate shut and barred it.

"When'd Williams come in?" Regan asked.

"About an hour ago. Just come off'n the rimrock, carrying a rifle, leading his pack mule." Curiosity got the best of Old Wad. "How come our bosom friend ride with you, Jim?"

"Hired him away from New Mexico Wagons."

Old Wad rubbed his scraggly hair, but said nothing. Dusk was thick, and Regan glanced at the mules grazing on the alfalfa roots. Old Wad climbed on his horse and filled him with details on the ride to the Williams' hacienda. He and Pedro already had had water running over one alfalfa field. The oldster looked tired and dishevelled. Regan guessed they'd done some hard shovelling on irrigation ditches.

"How's Williams taking it?" Regan asked.

"Doesn't seem excited."

"They tell he's batty as a deerfly in May," Morrison said.

"Don't look that way to me. Course, he could stand a bath, but all of us could take that, I reckon." He rubbed his bearded chin. "Had some company before Williams came, too. From town, this time —that fat sheriff."

"What'd he want?" Regan asked.

"He wouldn't tell me. Asked if you was around and when I said no he sat his horse for a while looking at our mules out grazing. I figure he was out scouting for New Mexico Wagons."

They rode to the buildings. Again Jim

Regan liked the looks of this spread—it had about everything he needed to operate from. They went down and Morrison said, "I'll put your horse away, boss," and led the horses into the barn.

Old Wad jabbed a thumb toward Morrison. "You really hired him, Jim?"

"New Mexico Wagons canned him."

"I wonder."

"I'll handle him," Jim Regan promised. He saw a lamp was lit in the house. "Williams in there?"

"Yeah."

Regan's spurs made tinkling sounds across the flagstone porch. His heart thundered against its rib cage and his blood hammered. Williams was sitting at the table, back to him, eating, as he entered. Regan never forgot his first sight of Enrique Williams.

Williams was a rangy bony man of about fifty. A faded blue chambray shirt, torn down the back, covered his shoulders and his lace-boots were old, scuffed and worn, as were his grey army pants. Jim Regan saw a long nose, a thin mouth, and whiskers, and behind these whiskers were dull blue eyes, eyes that now took in his every movement.

Williams got to his feet, shaking his head and sending his long shoulder-length grey hair twirling, like a girl does. He stuck out a bony claw.

"I take it you're Jim Regan?"

Regan shook hands; the claw fell. But the claw had had power and purpose. Regan sat down. "Welcome to my outfit." He emphasised the word *my*.

Williams sat down again. He had a plate of ham and fried potatoes in front of him and Jim Regan felt hunger suddenly gnaw on him, realising then how weary and saddle-tired and hungry he actually was.

"I was surprised," Williams said.

Regan apologised profusely. He needed this man's grass, this man's buildings, this man's good will. Upon this man's good will rested grass for his mules, a station for his freight outfit, bunks for his men. They sounded each other out with words.

Regan found himself thinking that this man was not stupid. He was a dreamer, his boots were not anchored in alfalfa roots he had inherited. He was back in the high Mogollons, moving through dangerous Apache country, searching for that will-of-the-wisp, a lost and fabulous and very rich gold mine.

"They call it the Lost Adam because it was found by a man named Jack Adam. He started for Silver City with a burro loaded with nuggets—raw gold, Mr. Regan. Apaches jumped him. But the strange thing was they never killed him."

Regan listened in raw impatience he kept hidden. He had heard similar wild tales many times before. "I wonder why. They usually kill every living thing."

Williams dug for a pipe that smelled like an open sewer line. He jammed raw tobacco into its stinking bowl.

"They just took Adam's gold and mule. They told him to get out and stay out. They took his water. He came in one night—that was about five years ago—blabbering and dying of thirst and starvation. He had both pockets full of nuggets. I've never seen a man so afraid in my life. He actually trembled three days afterwards."

Regan nodded. "Did he go back?"

Williams' hair shook. "Not Jack Adam. He told me roughly where the gold is, then pulled out for El Paso, and nobody's heard of him since." Williams dug in his pocket. He handed Regan an old gold coin. Regan squinted in the light. "I can't read what little print is on it."

"An old Spanish *real*, sixteenth century. Solid gold, Mr. Regan. He had a handful of them. He's found the hiding place of the padres." Regan noticed that Williams' voice had risen shrilly.

"You think you're close?"

"I'm on it, Regan, on it."

They all said that. They begged for grubstakes, they babbled for credit—one more trip and I'll have it. We'll both be rich. Christ, we'll roll in nuggets, we will!

"Where you going to freight to and from?" Williams asked, changing the subject in mid-air. "New Mexico Wagons has all Silver City—El Paso freighting sewed-up, they told me."

"Maybe into the Mogollons."

Williams' dull eyes pulled down. He sucked on the old pipe with noisy draughts. He reached under the table, fumbled, came out with a poke of gold, spilling nuggets on the table, the kerosene lamp glistening on raw gold.

Regan looked at him.

"Gold," Williams said, "and it can be yours."

Regan reined in curiosity. He judged about five thousand ore in that poke. "How?"

"By freighting grub into Mogollon."

Old Wad came in. "Morrison got some grub and is out irrigating." He looked at the gold. "Quite a mass of it. Biggest poke I've seen since that Black Hills prospector hit that lode down on Pine Crick."

"They're starving up there," Williams said. "Loaded with gold, but who can eat a nugget. Right in the middle of Apacheria, and they're eating goats, cats, dogs, burros."

"They rent you?" Regan asked, blood stirring.

"They did."

"How come you get through Apache scouts?" Old Wad asked.

"Like this," Williams replied.

Without warning he leaped to his feet. He tousled up his long hair. It hung in strings over his face like the hair of a witch. Through his hair his eyes glowed, rolling in red sockets. His gnarled hands were grabbing talons. Slobber rolled down his whiskery jaw. Suddenly he sat down and brushed back his hair. His eyes were smiling.

Regan said, "Maybe you could get us through?"

Williams shook his head. "They don't touch me. But you boys are sane, remember? You taking it?"

"No wagons."

"There're two old freight wagons in the shed behind the barn. They'll need grease and a few minor repairs. Supplies will cost around a thousand bucks. I got a list they sent out with me." He dug a soiled piece of wrapping paper out of a pocket. "That leaves four thousand or so for you. Couple of weeks work, Regan. Good pay."

Regan smiled bleakly. "Good pay?"

Williams continued with, "You got to have my ranch—or trail your mules out to God knows where. Hell, man, don't kid yourselves. Bill Sledge has the only other pasture that could feed your mules. And the de Cordovas have Sledge sewed up tighter than a bull's rearend in fly time!"

Regan nodded, saying nothing.

"Those people in Mogollon are starving. Men, women, little children, a few babies. They need cartridges, rifles, and grub. I'll lease my grass to you at your own price under one condition."

"That we freight into Mogollon?" Regan's eyes were on Williams. "You got near kin there?"

"No. But did you ever see a child starve? Either you freight to Mogollon— or I'll have the army run you off my land."

Williams' voice was shrill again.

Regan told about the abandonment of Fort Bayard.

Williams sank in his chair, eyes coals. "Then this country is at the mercy of Victorio and his killers. Heard that the Chiricahua Apaches have really raised hell over in Arizona. But didn't know it was so bad they'd pull Fort Bayard troops over there. What the hell us poor bastards supposed to do?"

"Get killed, I guess," Regan said mirthlessly.

Old Wad canted his ugly head. "Riders coming," he said.

Williams quickly killed the lamp. Regan wondered why he'd done this—Apaches didn't ride openly into a camp. This whole thing was crazy. Cockeyed as a turpentined rooster.

"You two go out," Williams said in a whisper.

Jim Regan and Old Wad walked outside. Two riders, one a heavy squat shadow, the other tall and narrow, came from the direction of Silver City, and now were about a hundred yards away, riding into the beginning of the buildings. Despite the deep twilight Jim Regan recognised them and walked down the steps, stopping as they came in.

Old Wad stayed in the dark of the long porch.

Jim Regan said, "You lookin' for me, Garcia?" He deliberately avoided using the word *sheriff*. He paid no attention to the other rider.

Garcia rode a grey mare. "Enrique Williams around?"

"Haven't seen him." Regan let his eyes move over the other rider, holding scorn. "You were out here once before today. My man said you asked about me. You got a warrant?"

"What if I did have?"

"You'd never serve it," Regan said. "Fort Bayard is gone, Garcia. There's no army to back you up now. New Mexico Wagons will have to freight out and in without the army boys now."

"I could get deputies."

Regan laughed quietly. "I've been in a

few saloons in town. I've heard them talk. You might get a few men to ride with you but none would be gringos. You Mexicans sort of forget one thing. This land is US Territory and Mexico doesn't own it any more."

"You never leased this place," Juan de Cordova said.

Jim Regan looked at the dandy. "How do you know I didn't?"

"No lease is recorded in the court-house."

"You get around," Regan said. "Maybe I'm not going to record it?"

"Then it wouldn't be legal."

Regan stepped forward one step. Juan de Cordova did not move back his sorrel. Regan stopped.

"Get over this idea of law and legal proceedings, de Cordova. The army's gone. Apaches are knocking on the door. The only law is now what a man packs in his fists or his rifle or his sidearm."

Sheriff Lucas Garcia said quickly, "Enough of this bickering. Williams ain't here, huh? Mind if we search the premises?"

"I sure do."

All the time he was pondering, wondering, guessing—why was this pair so hellbent to see Enrique Williams? Regan was no fool—he knew they didn't believe he'd leased this outfit. They knew he was bluffing. Evidently then they wanted to see Williams, get him to lease to New Mexico Wagons?

Juan de Cordova said, "He's as crazy as Williams. We come out looking for one crazy man and run into another."

Regan got the sorrel's reins, bunching them in a hard fist. "Say that again, de Cordova?"

Juan de Cordova put his weight on his left stirrup preparatory to swinging down, but Garcia reined in quickly, holding the freighter in saddle.

"Juan." Garcia's voice was low.

De Cordova hesitated, balanced on one boot. He hung that way for a long moment, face craggy and cold, then slowly moved back into his saddle.

Regan released the reins.

Without another word, Juan de Cordova and Garcia turned their horses, loping through the dusk toward the gate.

Regan stood for a moment in silence. His mind was busy, gathering this, discarding that, and finally it all revolved around these words: "He's as crazy as Williams. We come out looking for one crazy man and run into another." He went back into the dark house knowing then he had the answer.

"So that's why you doused the light?"

Williams nodded.

"Have they tried it before?"

"No, not that I know of."

"Then why now?" Regan answered that. "Because when a judge signs a warrant, the law picks up the man they say is loco. Then he has no legal right to sign contracts or make financial negotiations."

"And another reason," Williams said slowly. "They might figure I found the Lost Adam. And a crazy man would have no right to Lost Adam gold. Come daylight I'm getting me some grub and I'm pulling out again. I don't like steel bars."

His eyes found Regan's. Regan re-lit the lamp. William's eyes were clear and penetrating. His hands trembled as he scooped up the nuggets and restored them to the buckskin poke.

"Now you've got me over a barrel," Williams said. "If I appeal to de Cordova, I go to jail."

"We'll make the run," Regan said.

Williams slowly pushed the heavy poke toward him.

6

ABANDONMENT of Fort Bayard sent fingers of fear sneaking through Silver City. They met in groups, on streets and in houses talking of this danger. The protection of armed troops was gone. Gone was the security of the swift cavalry, sabres upraised. Gone was the security of the many rifles and pistols.

Hurriedly Juan de Cordova called the town council to session. Although Banker Jaime Lamas was by vote the mayor, Juan de Cordova was really the boss, something not displeasing to Senor Lamas, who was by nature not a leader—he was the spider, sitting in his bank, weaving his financial web.

Out of this hurried meeting came the decison to establish a town militia. Each night guards would be posted to hem in the town. Haste was urgent. Silver City sat poised on the brink of death surrounded by Apacheria. Sheriff Lucas Garcia was appointed to establish the militia.

Editor Joseph Cortinas sat at the rear of the smokefilled room, loafing in his chair. He listened but said nothing. Upon the appointment of Sheriff Lucas Garcia as commandante, Cortinas had to allow himself a tight smile. His imagination went to work. Across the screen of his mind they moved, this obese sheriff snapping orders in his wheezy voice, a motley crew of rag-a-muffins attempting to follow his squeaky orders.

Plans completed, there fell a short silence, each man on the council weighing this quick decision.

Cortinas waited for the opportune moment and then said, "I've dug back into old newspaper files, gentlemen. This would not be the first time Apaches have sacked and burned Silver City. About fifty years ago a similar event took place. The city burned for a number of days, and there was quite a slaughter."

Juan de Cordova turned quickly, mouth rimmed by hard lines. "Keep that to yourself! No use scaring our people still more!"

Cortinas thought, cynically, *Our people*, but said nothing. His point had been gained. He'd seen them all shiver.

Their eyes held for a moment. Juan de Cordova had a sudden cold feeling, for this man's words had held more than stated, and somehow he hooked this to the arrival of Jim Regan and his mules in this area.

Banker Lamas said, "No use fighting among ourselves, men." He laughed shakily. "Save that for those damn' Apaches."

Juan de Cordova snapped to Sheriff Garcia, "Get on this right away. Not a moment to spare. We have to have guards out tonight."

And the meeting was over.

Maria de Cordova awakened early the next morning. Her sleep had been broken, spattered by wild dangerous dreams. Scant daybreak found her lying in her huge bed looking at the ceiling. The cool morning breeze stirred the heavy Spanish drapes. Her dark eyes roamed over the room she had known since childhood.

She could hear Phillipa rattling pots and pans in the kitchen. Anger touched her—Phillipa was so noisy, so thoughtless of others . . . Why had she not been able to sleep? Why was she awake at this ungodly hour of five-fifteen?

Fort Bayard's protection gone. Apaches, painted, murderous, roaming the mountains, the desert. And this other trouble with Senor Regan . . . She remembered him, standing there, almost lifting her brother to his feet, their faces close together, each face dark with anger.

She thought, enough of such thoughts, and swung out of bed and stood up, her sheer nightgown clinging to her high-pointed breasts and firm full thighs. She ran water into the sunken tub and bathed, hearing boots pass outside on the gravel. The guard was changing. Overnight this hacienda had become a small fortress.

High walls surrounded it, made of thick rock, and Juan had had barbed wire strung around the top of the wall, and Juan had stationed retainers as guards, each man standing four hours.

Last night Juan had given her a terrible scolding. She and John Watson, a mining engineer, had driven out to Tres Ninos Springs, four miles north of town, on a picnic. She had been lying on her back, watching the stars, listening to the dull gurgle of the spring, when John had decided to make advances.

Even now she remembered his hands, trembling and hungry and damp, creeping up her full thighs, and she remembered his lips, hot and excited, crushing down on hers. For a moment passion had gathered, panting to spend itself, and then she had leaped to her feet, breasts rising and falling.

"We're going home, right now, John."

Angrily he had got to his feet, grabbed for her, but she danced out of reach, dress swirling to outline her hip. He tried again, missed, and then stood there, black anger on his handsome face.

"Damn it to hell, Maria, I believe you're a virgin."

"I am. And I'm not ashamed. I'm proud of it."

"You don't know what you've missed—"

"Oh, I think I do. When I marry, I'll make up for it."

"Will you marry me?"

"You won't get what you want that way," she said, and climbed into the buggy. The ride home was made in sullen disappointed silence. John had pulled the horse to a halt in front of the gate and said, "I'm through with you."

"Why, thank you for such good news."

She had hurried into the house. These *Americanos*—these gringo mine-owners and *engineros*—they were all the same. They wanted everything a girl—or this country—owned. Their talk was boring, about homes and women in the east, how they were here just to make some money, then back to civilisation—And she had thought of Jim Regan again.

Senor Regan was here to stay. He spoke Spanish as well, if not better than she did. There was no returning east for him, no further pushing west—he was going to make himself a part of Silver City. She remembered the slant of his tawny eyes, the lines around his mouth, and she knew that, with the arrival of Jim Regan in Silver City, Silver City had changed and she had changed, and this knowledge made her tremble slightly.

Juan awaited her. He grabbed her shoulders roughly, spinning her across the room, where she fell into a chair.

"You damn' stupid female! Going out in the country on a picnic with Apaches roaming and looking for whites to kill! And with that damn' gringo engineer! First thing you know you'll be walking around with a big belly!"

She came to her feet, white with rage. They faced each other in the huge room with its huge beams of native pine, with its thick adobe walls, its tiled floor, the stone fireplace.

"Do not insult me! I am twenty-two years of age! I know my own mind! I am not a girl and you are not my father! I'm a woman and you are merely my brother —my overbearing, scheming brother! Do not talk to me about morals—you who crawl in Beauvrais' whorehouse on your hands and knees in the back door! How much a month does the Madame pay you? They say you own a percentage in her brothel?"

Anger made his high cheekbones stand out. His mouth made motions, lips constricted, white teeth showing. For a moment deep fear hit her, and then she saw his shoulders sag.

"Please go to your room. In the morning we both shall be sorry."

She glared at the huge oil portraits on the wall. Mother, Father, Grandfather— back across centuries, people alien to her. She wanted to get an axe and knock them from the wall, pound them into glass and wood.

"I hate you all," she spat at the portraits.

Now she selected her blue skirt and green blouse, for the green complemented her red hair. She was proud of her red hair and she patted it into place, peering at her olive-skinned beauty in the tall mirror that had been her mother's, and before that her mother's mother's, and so back into years. She went to the big kitchen, where fat Phillipa had already cooked.

"We lived through another night." Phillipa crossed her ample bosom.

"Such talk."

She drank only coffee, black. She nibbled on a bit of toast but Phillipa could get her to eat no more. She walked through the garden, inspecting her roses, but she was not interested in them, and they did not smell sweet this morning. She had been rude to Phillipa. Phillipa was, in one sense, the only mother she'd ever known, for her mother had died when she, Maria, was five. And seventeen years is a long, long time. Five years now since her father had passed on; she had been seventeen and away in convent school.

She got Jose out of bed and he harnessed Estellita, her mare, to the buggy, and she drove toward Silver City, about one-half a mile down the hill, thinking of Juan and their violent quarrel. They had come close to a quarrel yesterday, too.

"You have been lucky so far. You've killed one freighter. You ran the others off. But I do not think you will kill, or run off, Senor Regan."

"Have I asked for your opinion?"

"No, but you will take it, regardless. You will blunder along, filled with grandiose power—you are a de Cordova, you know. Regan will not go; he is not like the others."

"I killed one, remember?"

"Yes, you did. His death is on your black soul, not mine. And for that I thank God."

Her words had hit him hard. Blood drained from his face, his fingers trembled, and without another word he'd turned and left the office, going to the barn and wagon-shed across the compound.

Anger, she'd thought, is a terrible foe. If only one could learn to control anger . . . and his tongue. She loved her brother—he was the only kin she had here—and she was afraid for him. One of their oilers, a wizened old man named Carlos, had told her that he knew of the Regans. He'd greased wagons for the elder Regan in Monterrey. He'd told her about the Maximilian Revolution driving the Regan company out of Old Mexico, how Regan's father had been killed by *revolucionarios* from ambush. He'd left out much and she had read between his lines.

She was standing by the window, gazing absently out on the street, when the two wagons moved across her vision, going north toward the business section, and with a start she saw one of the drivers, the one in the lead, was Jim Regan. He drove a high-wheeled Studebaker freight-wagon. He had two spans of mules, strung out, hitched to the wagon.

He sat on the high spring seat, boots on the footboard, bullwhip coiled behind him. His eyes met hers and she felt her face redden slightly, the small pulse at her throat leapt unexpectedly. Then he was out of the window's limit. The next wagon, she saw, was driven by Frank Morrison.

Where had he got the two wagons? Where the harness? What was he going to haul? Where was he going to haul to? These questions tumbled through her. She turned to the wall mirror, swept her glorious red hair into place, straightened her skirt across her hips, and went outside.

A few curious had gathered around the wagons which stopped before El Mercado, Valenzuela's store, which had just opened for the day. She noticed quickly that the mules were of good stock, high-legged with heavy shoulders, and then she took her eyes to Jim Regan, climbing down from his wagon. Regan went into the store.

Regan had also spent a restless night. Many problems had darted through his mind seeking answers. Each turn of a wheel on this trip would be freighted heavily with danger. First he pondered on taking which one—Old Wad or Frank Morrison—on this trip. He had finally settled on Morrison, unknown quality which he was. Old Wad was too old.

He realised Old Wad was jealous of Morrison, fearing Morrison would push himself into the limelight. It was the jealousy of an old man, strangely akin to the jealousy of an old gossipy woman. This solution reached, he'd turned his mind to a more pressing problem—how to crack the shell of freighting in Silver City.

Somewhere there had to be a crevice into which he could insert a crowbar. One by one he went over the list of faces—the people he'd met and talked to in Silver City. He immediately disqualified the banker, Jaime Lamas. Lamas was a fat, tail-wagging dog. He would go wherever and to whoever paid him the most profit. Sheriff Lucas Garcia also did not dwell long in his mind. Garcia was a puppet, nothing more. Matthew Valenzuela was a merchant, out to make money. Regan remembered his slow thoughtfulness, his listening attitude, his slight hesitation. Then he decided that Valenzuela did not have the potential crevice for the crowbar.

He outlawed the mine owners and superintendents, too. They were making riches hand over fist. They were of Spanish extraction and this blood, coupled with long association, would hold them to New Mexico Wagons.

That left only one man. Editor Joseph Cortinas.

His deductions were simple. Cortinas owned the newspaper, the only newspaper. Through it Cortinas could control the thinking of this town. Regan knew full well the naked power of the press. Cortinas might offer the chink.

Accordingly, his mind cleared, he went to sleep, but he was up at dawn, wheeling the wagons out of the shed. Williams had gone during the night, a wraith who had tarried, done his work, and now was slipping back into the pines, searching for his fabulous fortune. Pedro came in, face weary from the night watch. The mules were safe.

"No Indians."

Regan said, "Get eight of the best mules. Those with the most flesh, our toughest. Don't leave out Sweet Jasmine."

"What you do?"

"Freight."

Pedro asked nothing more. He got a rawhide riata, eight halters, and went out into the pasture, coming back with eight mules. By this time Regan, Morrison, and Old Wad had the wagons out. Regan saw they were old but strong of beams and reach. They greased them. They found harnesses, covered with thick dust, hanging in a shed. They slapped these on the mules.

Wad and Regan were to one side. Old Wad asked, "I go with you, I suppose." More of a statement than a question.

Regan used a white lie. "I can trust you," he said quietly. "I do not know Morrison well. For all I know he might be a spy for New Mexico Wagons. I can keep him under my eye if he goes with me."

Old Wad rubbed his beard and said, "A wise decision," and let it go at that, and Regan let breath from his lungs. But still the bigger part was still there, two men alone with two hundred mules, and Apaches wanted roast mule meat.

He spoke to Frank Morrison. "You're going with me. Are you afraid?"

Morrison's swollen lips smiled crookedly. "Hell, I'm not good at lying. Christ, yes, I'm afraid."

"You don't have to go."

"I'll be along."

Regan looked at him. Morrison looked at Regan. Then Morrison laughed and slapped him on the back. "Who t'hell wants to live forever?" They both laughed and went to work. But Regan found himself wondering if Morrison was not trying to get back at Juan de Cordova.

He could not believe this, for Morrison seemed purely without guile. He was not a leader, he was a follower—he'd tie his line to the wagon of the right leader, and he'd die for that man. Years in handling men of all ages, colors, and backgrounds had taught Regan much about his fellow men.

Finally Morrison went up, gathering his ribbons, leaned back and said "Hell, I'm ready for Victorio," and boomed out his loud laugh.

Regan got Old Wad to one side. "See that third post in the corral on the side closest to us?"

"Yes?"

"I buried that five thousand gold there."

Old Wad nodded, wetting his cracked lips. "You'll be back, Jim." His face twisted suddenly, and he walked away.

Now Regan showed Valenzuela the list Williams had given him. "Where you hauling this?"

"Mogollon."

Valenzuela studied him, and Regan

searched for the first crevice. He had his crowbar ready.

"Did I hear right, *Senor* Regan?"

"You did, Mogollon."

Valenzuela's dark Spanish eyes were on him. Other eyes were on him. Was this gringo loco? Had the heat hit him?

"They're starving up there," Regan said.

"I've heard that," Valenzuela said, eyes now on the list. "I heard they tried to get New Mexico wagons to haul—" He stopped suddenly. "Drive your wagons around back to the alley. We'll load there from the warehouse."

Regan went out into the sunshine that was gathering warmth, promising a warm desert fall day. At this moment a group of men, marching in ragged military fashion, rifles over their shoulders, came around the corner, accompanied by Sheriff Lucas Garcia and his wheezing *one two three*. They marched by, a complement of about thirty men, all ages and colors, led by the obese sheriff, and Regan looked at the

111

man standing beside him, who turned out to be Editor Cortinas.

"The War's been over fourteen years. Lee surrendered to Grant at Appomattox. The South will rise again."

Cortinas was cynical. "Our army. Apache killers, every one of them. Every bottle is a dead Apache." He added. "Town council orders." He looked at the wagons. "Where t'hell are you going?"

Regan told him the same story he'd told Valenzuela. Cortinas circled him warily in his mind and asked, "And who's paying you for this?"

"I'm footing the bill."

Cortinas inhaled deeply. "That is hard to believe." He put up a palm suddenly. "No, I'm not serious, Senor Regan." Regan could sense his mind working— the mind of a reporter, an editor, a man in search of a story. He took a newspaper out of his coat pocket. "Just off the press, still fresh ink. Your ad is there and you're on the front page."

Regan knew that publicity, even if bad, was still good, for it brought a man's name and character to thousands of people. Although Cortinas did not say it, he knew that next issue he would be again on the front page. Cortinas stepped back. "I'll interview you when you come back. That is, *if* you come back."

"Thanks." Regan spoke thinly.

Cortinas seemed speaking to himself. "A newcomer, buffeted around town, not welcome, on his own hook—with his own money—going to transport supplies to Mogollon, right through Apacheria. Cristo, if I could only get to a wire this would hit headlines all over the US. Army pulls out, leaves town to death under Apache war-axes, to starve to death, Silver City will do nothing. New Mexico Wagons sits on dead ass, secured to death. God, if I could only get to a wire." He turned without good-bye and went to his office.

Regan thought, The first crack. Crowbar, stay poised. He called to Sheriff Garcia, who had halted his squad fifty feet away. The sheriff came over, scowling deeply.

"What do you want?"

Regan told him about Mogollon. He deliberately raised his voice because now Juan de Cordova stood in the gathering. "I'm leaving my mules on Williams' grass. The old man—Old Wad Emerson—and Pedro are the only two with them. I'm laying those mules—and the fate of my men—in your hands."

Garcia's cheekbones were pale. "What do you mean by that?"

Mexicans are usually short people. Because of this Jim Regan could look across the heads and meet Juan de Cordova's eyes.

"You're sheriff here, Senor Garcia. Your job is to protect my men, my mules, and my property."

"Not against Apaches." Garcia spoke hurriedly.

"I'll waive a point there. But you can protect them against *white* Apaches."

Juan de Cordova smiled thinly. Sheriff Garcia turned, following Regan's eyes, and he saw de Cordova. "There'll be no white Apaches," he wheezed.

Regan had what he wanted. The fat sheriff had committed himself before many witnesses. Sheriff Lucas Garcia apparently became suddenly aware of this. He turned, back straight, a ludicrous figure, and marched stiff-legged back to his *company*.

Juan de Cordova stood rooted. Regan saw eyes swing to him, then hurriedly pull away. Valenzuela stuck his head out of the store's door. "Get your wagons in the back, please."

They drove around the block and came down the alley to the loading platform. Regan noticed that Frank Morrison rode high on his seat, bullwhip crackling needlessly. He smiled.

Valenzuela had three Mexicans carrying materials from the store-room. Regan and Morrison gave instructions on placing the load. Tinned goods went on the bottom, evenly distributed to provide even weight, and soft goods went on top, except for the case of five rifles and the ammunition.

"Those rifles will look good to those red-skinned bastards," Valenzuela said.

"Why not put them on the bottom where they can't be seen?"

"We might need them," Regan said.

Regan walked around and tested the off-rein on his lead mule. He became aware suddenly that Maria de Cordova stood beside him. She had come through the space between the Mercado and the next building.

He felt his blood quicken. His fingers trembled on the mule's bit. He remembered the first time he'd seen her, standing there in the doorway of New Mexico Wagon's office—the day he'd shaken Juan de Cordova's back teeth. His mental vision was complete—the small, olive-skinned girlish face, the glistening red hair, her thin waist and womanly softness.

He looked down.

She smiled at him. He liked the little crinkles at the corner of her mouth, and his eyes saw the full rise of her breasts. The green of her blouse accentuated her dark skin, giving added gleen to her healthy red hair.

Her dark eyes met his.

This man had changed somewhat, since she had first seen him. Then he had a more boyish mouth more ready to laugh, she thought, but now he was serious, suntanned face graven and almost austere, a trifle older than his years. She could only guess. She had not known him long—but less than a week. There was something about him, some masculine quality, that was deadly, but still attractive. She had the out-of-place thought that he would be kind, considerate, good, to the woman he loved.

Her voice was throaty. "You are a brave and good man, Senor Regan."

Regan wondered, dully, if she could hear his heart beat. He said, in a low voice, "I thank you, Senorita de Cordova."

Suddenly she stood on tiptoe. To his surprise she kissed him lightly on the cheek—a mere whisp of her lips, yet warm and wholesome. Then she smiled and was gone, a thistle down moving out of sight between the two buildings.

Regan's gnarled fingers came up and softly touched his cheek. Then he came to earth and glanced around to see if anybody had watched. Nobody had followed them into the alley, though. Frank Morrison had seen, though, for he had been at the end of the rear wagon, stacking his load. Regan glanced at him but the man's face showed nothing. Regan got another glimpse into this man Morrison—a bit of good breeding, some trace of finery the rough frontier had not completely erased.

"We're ready to move," Morrison said, and climbed on his high seat.

Regan wrote a check for Valenzuela. Cyncism returned and he said, "I've got ten thousand oro in Senor Lamas' bank."

Valenzuela's olive skin went darker. Regan thought, Hell, my words might have closed the chink. Valenzuela did not glance at the sum on the check. He said merely, "Good luck," and walked back into his store.

"You put his back up," Morrison said.

Regan had no reply. He went up,

springs settled, and his bullwhip talked, curled, popping, over the mules. The hours of rest and alfalfa—although the latter had been sparse and short—had done wonders. Mules hit collars, wheels moved, and Regan settled back, finding again contentment in straining mules, high lumbering wheels, the sway of a freight wagon.

They made one stop before their first camp at noon. That was beside the high gate from which Regan's bullets had blasted Williams' padlock. Morrison stayed in his seat. Regan walked into the brush and came back with two small wooden cartons. He gave one to Morrison.

"You sure you know how to use this stuff?"

"I've worked in mines," Morrison said simply.

7

THE old man leaned on his long-barrelled Sharps rifle. "So them sojer boys pulled outa Fort Bayard, eh? Got cold feet, I reckon. That should raise the price them merchants are payin' for Apaches. How much they puttin' out for an Apache now?"

Regan was unhitching his mules. Because of the late start they had made only sixteen miles and were at Agua Fria Springs on the west slope of the Pinos Altos mountains.

"Two hundred and fifty bucks, Mr. Reynolds."

Reynolds whistled between scraggly teeth. "Almost double the price, eh? Them scissorbills really must be fillin' their drawers. Sold 'em two about three weeks ago. Only one-fifty a head then."

Frank Morrison asked, "How many you got, Reynolds?"

"Four of 'em, the bastards. I'm keepin' 'em whole back in a cave in the hill."

"No need to keep the carcass," Morrison said. "They pay for the scalp just as good as for the entire carcass."

"Last time I had to tote the carcasses in," Reynolds said. "Stank like skunks. After supper I'll lift me some hair an' throw the meat into a coulee for the buzzards."

Reynolds turned and went toward the adobe house set in the clearing surrounded by gnarled live-oaks. Regan saw him stick his bearded head into the doorway and holler out some Spanish to whoever was inside, evidently the old man's present wife. Regan and Morrison were surrounded by bug-eyed children of all sizes and ages. Some had evidently forgotten to put on their breech-cloths.

This mystified Regan. Morrison had freighted over this road for New Mexico Wagons before the Apache uprising. He claimed that Reynolds and his Mexican wife were the only adults at Agua Fria Springs.

"Who owns all those children, Morrison?"

Morrison shrugged. "Old Reynolds. The four years I've been around here he's had at least a wife a year. Sometimes he has two or three at the same time." Morrison peeled harness from a mule. "Some Mexican, some 'pache." Morrison slipped a halter on the mule's ugly head. "He must be eighty if he's a day. Regular human stud horse."

They watered the mules at the spring. It was a good spring, throwing lots of cold water, and it ran about a hundred yards, then suddenly seemed to get tired and disappeared in the sand. Before Victorio had broken off the Mescalero with his braves New Mexico Wagons had run a weekly freight wagon to Mogollon. They'd fed night-stop at Agua Fria and therefore there was some de Cordova hay in the small feed-lot behind the barn. Their mules watered, they tied their mules to the feed-rack beside the barbed-wire fence of the lot, shoving alfalfa hay into the mangers. They had some ground barley in their wagons and they doled out proper measures of this into the grain boxes. The mules were fixed for the night . . . unless Apaches raided.

Agua Fria Springs lay on the flat of a coulee. West the coulee ran out into the desert. The side-hills to the other directions were cleared of chamiso and manzinita and other brush. Grub hoes and axes had cut down all brush to the top of the hills. To sneak up on the Springs, Apaches would have to cross barren strips of ground.

"Wonder how he grubbed off all this brush?" Regan asked.

"His kids. He keeps them working."

"More than my old man could make me do," Regan said with a smile. At that moment Old Reynolds stuck his bearded head out of the door of the house. "Chuck is on, boys."

Reynold's present wife was a heavy young Mexican woman who couldn't speak a word of English. Regan expected the table to be crowded with children but such was not the case—Reynolds and

Morrison and he ate alone. A full grown girl of about sixteen, evidently one of Reynold's daughters, served the table, darting out occasionally carrying trays of food, and Regan guessed the children ate outside at the long table under the live-oaks.

The girl was a little beauty. Dark hair, glistening and healthy, framed a full face. Huge shell ear-rings hung to her small ears and her eyes were very dark, sparkling with life. She was fully matured with ripe breasts, a thin waist, and rather wide hips. She smiled at Regan, but he did not smile back. Once he saw Morrison wink at her and she winked back, glancing at Reynolds, but the old frontiersman was nose-deep in his victuals.

Regan guessed she was lonely.

Meal finished, Regan strolled outside, smoking a Sweet Caperal, one of the new-fangled tailor-made cigarettes. He was slowly rubbing salve on a mule's shoulder when the girl went by.

"I'm going swimming," she said.

Regan could hear the children down in

the live-oaks; evidently they were in swimming. There was something subtle here, something he couldn't quite pin down. The girl did not carry a bathing-suit. The wind moved against her cotton dress, showing its endearment by making the dress hug a nice thigh.

Regan merely nodded.

"I don't swim with the children, though. I swim below them, in a bigger pool."

Regan caught the signficance then. He said, "That's nice," and continued his slow rubbing, for the mule's shoulder was threatening to gall. When he looked up again, the girl had left. Morrison had just come out of the house. He looked at Regan, then at the girl, and sat down on the bench. About five minutes later, Regan looked up and the bench was empty.

Reynolds occupied Morrison's place. His mules comfortable, Regan walked over and sat beside Reynolds. Reynolds sucked on a pipe almost as foul-smelling as Enrique Williams'.

"Morrison takes guard until midnight. Then I take from there to dawn. We want breakfast at the crack of daylight."

Reynolds nodded. "No need for guard." He jabbed his pipe toward a live-oak tree. "I got a little cabin up there. Can't see it because of them thick leaves." He jabbed at the terrier sitting beside him. "Constantinople and me sleep up there. Constantinople hates 'paches worse 'n skunks. One come inside a half mile an' he growls."

"How many've you killed?"

"You mean in the twenty odd years I bin here? Hell, I dunno. Couldn't make an honest guess. Killed a heap even afore there was a bounty on them. They sneak in across that place where they ain't no brush—boom goes ol' Sharpy an' I got another."

His voice held no malice. He talked with the casual tone of a hunter telling about shooting ducks.

"So New Mexico Wagons is ascared to make the Mogollon run, eh? Well, don't sell that Juan short, Mr. Regan."

Regan nodded, half asleep.

Reynolds knocked the doodle out of his foul pipe and got to his feet. "Reckon I better go up to the cave an' skin out them scalps. Wanna come along to see a kilt injun?"

That was the last thing Regan wanted to see, either dead or alive. "I'm going to hit the hay. You figure out what I owe you and I'll pay you at daybreak. Or I can pay you when we come back this way."

"Wait till you come back."

Regan looked at his dusty boots. "We might not get back."

"Then I'll collect it in hell. With 'pache hides payin' these prices, even if I don't collect it, it'll not break my wallet." Reynolds spoke to a boy of about six who stood listening. "Come along with your pappy, Matthew, an' watch the fun."

Old man and young boy started up the hill. Regan went to his wagon, took down his bedroll, unrolled it under the wagon, kicked off his boots, laid his hat and rifle beside the bed, and crawled in. He'd not had a night of full sleep for what seemed months, and weariness was not only in his flesh—it had burrowed deep into his bones. He wondered how Old Wad and Pedro were getting along with the mules and irrigation. He thought of Enrique Williams, out in these mountains, hair long and filled with cockle-burrs, searching for a mirage. He remembered dimly hearing Morrison and the girl returning from the—creek, and then he remembered nothing.

The roaring boom of the Sharps brought him upright. He bumped his head on the wagon-reach, grabbed his rifle and crawled out, then squatted beside the right front wheel, eyes probing the night. A quarter moon was up, giving off yellow light.

A glance told him his mules were all right. Crouched over, he ran barefooted for the live-oak grove, but no bullets came and he reached the grove's dark security. He swung his rifle as a form materialised ahead, and then he recognised Frank Morrison.

"I got me two hundred and fifty bucks."

The words came from the tree above. Regan could barely make out the outlines of Reynolds' tree-cabin.

Morrison said, "I was watching that strip. I never saw nobody move on it."

"He never got on the strip. I was sound asleep, an' then Constantinople growled. I saw him just on the edge of the brush. You look close you can see his carcass now—right below that big manzinita tree."

Regan heard Morrison exhale loudly. That took Morrison off the hook. "You going up after him?" Morrison asked.

"Hell, no. You think I'm loco. Where there's one there's always at least one more—they never travel alone. I walk up there an' I'd never come back. He'll be a little bloated by daybreak, but you can't bloat his scalp."

Regan's blood was a little cold. He and Morrison walked to the wagon. They bunkered in its protective shade. Regan said, "We should get these children out of here into Silver City. This fool had no sense of danger."

"I guess that's because he's lived in it all his life. We'll try on our way back. That is, *if* we get back—and the kids are here, *if* we get back."

Regan had no answer.

"You should've tried out that Conchita girl," Morrison said quietly. "She told me she invited you, too."

Regan felt a stiffness. There was much he could say, but what was the use—he let it ride. "Too damn' old," he joked.

They left at daybreak, fed, mules fresh, Regan almost his old self again, most of the deep-bred fatigue gone. Eastern mountains were dark, sunlight hit their peaks, throwing long shadows, dappled and blue, still clinging to darkness, and then the sun was on them, driving the yellow before it, and it blazed down, hinting of a hot noon.

The wagon road was well cleared, dipping over hills to run into gravel washes, these washes holding flimsy grey ghost trees with an occasional old cottonwood fighting for water and a hold on the flinty soil. Always the desert stretched on their left, for they were skirting the toe of the Pinos Altos, and would do so until they reached their next stop, which was the Santa Margarita Rancho, on the Gila River.

Morrison had explained the road carefully. "Then we leave the Santa Margarita —our big pull is clearing the north bank of the Gila—and its pretty level run then until our night camp, Horse Springs, right below the big bend of the San Francisco. Next morning we start the climb, because we follow the San Francisco to Mogollon."

"That last day? What kind of a road is it?"

"Right up San Francisco River Canyon, Regan. We swing back and forth, crossing the river a number of times. There's no danger in the river because it is low—this drought—"

"If they did hit," Regan said slowly. "They'd hit in the Canyon, you think?"

"Yes, if they do—that's the logical spot."

"We're using a lot of *ifs*."

"These Apaches don't fight like Sioux or other Plain Indians. They sometimes use the Comanche Wheel, but that's only when they hit on the desert and have lots of horse room. They fight from the rocks and brush and they're experts at camouflage. I've seen dead ones with their bodies painted green."

Regan glanced at him. "You mention Sioux. You ever been jumped by Sioux?"

"Freighting from Fort Benton to Great Falls, up in Montana Territory. And I've seen Comanches, too, freighting into Fort Hill." Morrison had turned suddenly to look at a mule's sweatrug. Regan'd got the impression he'd said too much.

Here was a steep grade and Regan dropped to the ground, carrying his Winchester, landing on the left side of his freighter. Morrison came down, too, and walked even with him, letting his dusty mules plod along, reins hooked over the brake handle.

"That injun that Reynolds killed." Morrison spoke slowly. "He had company. Like Reynolds said, they don't travel alone."

"They know we're here."

Morrison's dusty square face broke in a slow smile. "They must think we're as loco as Enrique Williams. Two men alone, two wagons loaded with supplies they need."

"Hope they think we're so crazy they won't touch us."

"Wishful thinking." Morrison dropped back to his rig. Regan let his thoughts roam. Twenty-nine years is not long for a man to live, but sometimes twenty-nine can seem like a hundred. He remembered Eleanor—their stormy five months of marriage. He thought of her light blondeness, her Nordic lightness of skin; the last time he'd seen her, she was dancing in the Crystal Palace in Deadwood, almost naked. Now why did he think of a woman he'd not seen for four years, now divorced from him? A man made mistakes. But memory was a fickle thing, never completely hiding its facts, as much as a man tried. He was glad they'd had no children.

Dimly, back in the dark recesses of his mind, he knew why he now thought of Eleanor, the sad and tragic and lost Eleanor, and it was because of Maria de Cordova.

He saw her again in the screen of his mind—her glowing red hair, the green blouse stressing her womanhood subtly, the tan skirt hugging her smooth thighs. He saw the slow start of her girlish smile, the little crinkles around her mouth, the slightly puggish nose, the dark eyes that could hold running merriment, or switch to cold disregard. She was woman and he was man, and the endless stirrings of millions of years, and years even beyond a million, were upon them, within them, part of them—because she was woman and he man. She had stood on tiptoe, magnificent body arched, breasts out and beautiful and she had kissed him hurriedly, a mere touch of warm lips, and then the wind had come in, sweeping her away with down-swiftness.

Morrison's bellow broke his thoughts short. "Laguna water hole in the draw below, boss."

They unhitched, mules drank from the green-scummed mudhole, they rested an hour, and then pushed on again—weary mules, dust-grimed, weary men, also thick with alkali whiteness. Again, the roaring hot sun, the plodding mules, a man walking beside his wagon to lighten the load. The sun heeled over, a ridge was ahead, beyond it, so Morrison said, was Santa Margarita Rancho. At Santa Margarita would be hay, grain, rest—a man always thought of his mules first. And there would be grub, company, talk.

And Apaches in the brush.

Heads down, fighting the grade, the mules dug in, eyes straining, slobber, rope-like, from gaping mouths. Then the ridge was gained. Regan saw a creek below them, its bed interspersed with brackish waterholes, and to his right slightly, was a grove of cottonwoods, and here the hacienda would be—but it was not there.

Regan said, "Whoa, boys," and the mules stopped instantly, heads down. He heard Morrison's boots grind towards him, then stop. He heard Morrison's deep drawn breath. And Morrison said, "Oh, God. Oh, God."

"Only the adobe walls standing."

"Adobe can't burn," Morrison said uselessly. He turned dust-red eyes on Jim Regan. "Where do we camp tonight?"

"Down where there's water," Regan said, also uselessly.

After they'd watered their mules they fed them measures of ground feed, pouring it in mounds on the ground. Regan said, "There's a little tule grass along the creek. We'll feed them there—not much, but better than nothing—but we don't unharness."

They ate out of tins. Then in the dusk, always carrying rifles, they looked over the wreckage. Regan realised this had once been a big rancho. Probably at least two hundred years old, built by some

Spanish grandee on his land grant given by the far-away King of Spain.

Adobe walls were at least three feet thick, a brown mass of mud, straw and native lime. Red tiled roofs had fallen, heavy timbers burned. Three huge mastiffs lay dead, one pin-cushioned with arrows. The Apaches had left not a living thing.

Morrison said, "Only two times I've heard the Apaches have left living people after a raid. Once was some thirty years ago when they jumped the Oatman wagons east of Yuma, right behind where the Gila meets the Colorado. They took two girls, one died, and years later the Mojaves turned the other loose at Fort Yuma, and she wanted to stay with the Indians—the Apaches had traded her to the Mojaves."

"The other?"

"When they let this Adam fellow live, the one that found the gold cache that this loony, Williams, is searching for. He come into Silver City gibbering like a hot-ironed ape. I reckon they figured he was loco and wanted nothing to do with him, like they figure Enrique Williams."

Jim Regan reconstructed this rancho in his mind. A huge rambling ranch house, complete with many angles, a long porch its length, flagstoned floored. Huge barns, corrals, blacksmith shop, bunkhouse for hands, a small city here in the desert-mountainous wasteland.

"They lifted lots of scalps," Morrison said. "You know, I can't even see a bone in that wreckage. They killed first, then heaved in bodies, and then torched the spread."

"Who owned it?"

"Oh, some damn' Spanish don, of the same high good-for-nothing blood that the de Cordovas have. I forget his name. I saw him once or twice, all dressed in old Spanish dress, wide-bottomed pants and all that. He looked right through this old gringo and never saw him. When we made camp here, it was always down by the water. Us freighters weren't good enough to walk in his yard."

Regan thought back to his first meeting

with Juan de Cordova. How the grandee had sat there, lips thin and cynical, almost saying aloud, "I don't want to waste time talking to you, you stupid gringo. I'm the son of a don and you're a son of a stupid Irishman and your mother was probably a peasant maid." Then he remembered Maria standing on tiptoe, the brush of her lips, the softness of her breath. The gringo, he voiced grimly, was here, and the gringo was here to stay—even if they had to bury him to make him stay permanently. He took his mind from such thoughts. They were not too healthy. His father had reared him to the American theory that all men were born equal and would remain equal until one showed the other otherwise.

He felt the ashes. They were cold, but Morrison kicked into a pile of debris, revealing a few hot coals. Evidently the furniture had been made of wood for there was little iron work showing in the wreckage. When the troops had deserted Fort Bayard, they'd given these Apaches an open licence to kill and rob and burn.

"Must've hit it about yesterday afternoon," Morrison said. "Well, nothing we can do here—do I stand first guard or second?"

"Which do you want?"

Morrison looked sharply at him. "Don't forget you're the boss, Regan."

They looked at each other. Two days with wagons and their clothes were dirty with grey dust and axle-grease. The scab had left the cut on Morrison's face. His whiskers, already tinged with grey, failed to cover the jagged scar on his right jowl, the livid slash that ran from eye socket to jaw. His nose, broken by Regan's fists, had healed a little crooked, giving him the air of a buccaneer, and a cutlass in his sash would have fitted his character perfectly.

Regan's black eye was slowly disappearing. Morrison had handed him that when his knuckles had ripped in savagely like steel pistons. The cut on the inside of his bottom lip still made his lip bigger than normal. A damn' weird and queer world, Regan thought. You beat a man half to death, after that you bend your Colt's barrel over his skull, and here you stand with him in a narrow draw holding the ruins of a once great rancho, and you grin at each other, like there'd never been anything but accord and peace between you.

"You made me pick up your hat, remember?"

Suddenly, Regan laughed. Morrison was laughing too, mouth open, tongue red. You had no reason to laugh. Here was this man—the man you beat the hell out of—and here you were, still wearing a black eye he'd given you, and for no reason under God's sun, you were both laughing.

"I'll take first hitch, Morrison, if it's okay with you?"

"You made me pick up the hat," Morrison repeated.

He walked away, laughing.

8

SLOWLY mass hysteria left Silver City. Even the extraordinary becomes common-place after a length of time. Sheriff Lucas Garcia's vigilantes increased rapidly in number for two days, and then enlistments suddenly petered out. Garcia had his oldest boy, the one who read the best English, search the meagre school library for history books. He found only one book that even referred to the attack Apaches had made on Silver City years before.

He had hoped to find a careful account of the battle. He talked with the oldest Father in the Mission, but learned nothing. Fathers came and went; the oldest, in point of service, had been at the Mission only eleven years.

Finally he had to turn to the morgue in Editor Cortinas' newspaper office. At first the whole thing was a hodgepodge—he could not find what he wanted. Cortinas wiped his ink-stained hands on his leather apron and quickly found the information. Garcia did not thank him. Garcia did not like this flippant newspaper man.

Once safe at home, Garcia gave the clippings long and diligent perusal, hoping to gain from them information that would help him map out a defence campaign.

Juan de Cordova called another town council meeting the third night after Regan and Morrison had creaked wagons out of town heading for Mogollon. Again he roughly overstepped the powers of Banker Lamas, the elected mayor. By this time Lamas was getting rather immune to de Cordova going over his head. He sighed, realising he was only a stooge. Like Sheriff Garcia.

Each of the mill-owners attended this meeting also. They too were of old Spanish blood, the ruling hierarchy. Their predecessors had owned and operated these mills and mines for many years.

One mine owner could even trace his proud lineage back to the blood of Hernando Cortez.

Editor Cortinas also attended, but not as a council member, but as a representative of his newspaper. Although he could, if he wanted to, prove that he also came from a proud old Spanish family, he was never really accepted into the hierarchy. He was tolerated but not welcomed. Sometimes his cynicism got the better of his logic. Actually they were afraid of his intelligence.

Lamas called the meeting to order, but it was Juan de Cordova who ran it. The seriousness of the situation rode on all shoulders. Not a man there had a desire to see his family murdered, his home burned, his own hair lifted. Silver City was a rich prize surrounded by murdering savages, abandoned by the armed forces to shift for itself.

"The first topic to be considered," Juan de Cordova said, "is the protection of our families, our persons, and our fortunes." He looked carefully about, noticing that

Sheriff Lucas Garcia was not in the meeting-room, the office of the bank. "Has anybody any suggestions?"

One of the mine owners stood up. "I move we drop everything but day shifts at the mills and mines. That way the men who are not working can be available for guard duty. And besides, what good is gold or silver if you can't get it out to market?"

Editor Cortinas saw Juan de Cordova frown at the last sentence. It's a reflection upon his freighting business, he thought, and when anything reflects upon any of his possessions, it actually is a reflection upon himself personally. Pride, false and stupid, holds that man together.

Juan de Cordova was immaculately dressed. He wore a dark brown suit of finest Habana cloth, hand tailored in Mexico City. His shirt was snow white, his tie glistening black, and his riding boots were black, shining in the dim light of the hanging kerosene lamp. Lamplight accentuated the high cheekbones, the thin lips, the piercing black eyes with their heavy brows.

The other mine owners were in agreement. The motion was passed. Merchant Valenzuela cleared his throat.

"Of course, these men laid-off will continue to draw wages from the mines, I presume?"

"Why should they?" a mine owner grunted testily. "They're in this mess with us, too. Apaches hit and they'd lose their hair, too."

"Things have changed in the last few years since the mines have been reopened, *senores*. Silver City is not all Spanish-speaking now. Some of these miners speak English and foreign tongues. They have some queer ideas regarding the working man and the employer. Some very radical ideas, I must admit—I hear them talk in my store, you know. With no wages coming in they might even desert Silver City."

Faces fell. Such a prospect could come about. The miners could form a tough armed body and hike across the desert to

El Paso, protected en route from Apache attack by their huge numbers. And if this happened, Silver City would be more susceptible to Apache attack, easier to destroy.

They hurriedly decided to pay each miner a full day's pay, and add on one dollar if he served in the militia.

Juan de Cordova studied the list lying on the desk. He seemed hesitant. Cortinas smiled inwardly. He knew what worried the immaculately dressed business man. Cortinas came willingly to his rescue.

"Do you honestly think that Sheriff Garcia is man enough to handle the militia and the defence of this town, if this defence becomes needed?"

There it is, Cortinas thought with sour glee. I took the bastard off the hook. Now watch him belly-ache and bellycrawl.

De Cordova's brown eyes rested on him warily. "Senor Garcia has been sheriff for many years. He has always ably maintained law and order. He even ran Billy Boney out of Silver City after Boney killed the blacksmith with a knife, claiming the man was molesting Billy's mother."

Nobody spoke. Each knew full well what was transpiring. Juan de Cordova—and his father before him—had always used Garcia as a stooge.

"Sheriff Garcia did something there that Sheriff Pat Garrett cannot do up in Lincoln County. I hear Billy the Kid is raising hell for Garrett."

Cortinas snorted. "Garcia never ran out Billy Boney. He left of his own accord."

"A debatable point," murmured Juan de Cordova.

They discussed this point, nonetheless, and the summation was to hire an ex-general from Juarez's Mexican army, one General Humberto Gonzalez, who had retired in Silver City. Sheriff Garcia, of course, would still be sheriff, a figure-head of the militia, but General Gonzalez would train the militia and, if battle came, would assume full command. Banker Lamas was appointed a committee of one to contact both Gonzalez and Garcia. Juan de Cordova stressed that the situation would demand the utmost tact.

They then turned to other matters, all pertaining to the town's defence. How many sidearms—also shotguns and rifles —were in Silver City? How much ammunition for these arms? How was the town treasury standing up—two hundred and fifty bucks was a large sum for an Apache scalp. Why?

"The treasury *has to* stand this price," a mine-owner stated flatly.

Cortinas noticed that Juan de Cordova did not enter this phase of the talk. He sat behind the big desk, with his eyes moving from man to man. He's got them under his thumb, every man-jack of them, the editor thought. Every one of them, to a man, owes his bank money. Through that bank he is going to run Jim Regan out of town. They won't dare ship out freight and haul in freight on Regan wagons. Not when de Cordova's bank holds their paper and can foreclose at a moment's notice.

By careful calculation, based upon his wide knowledge of this town and its people, he came to the conclusion that, of all the business men gathered here, he was the only one who did not owe Juan de Cordova's bank. Everything he had, his home, his shop, his equipment, was free of debt.

He wondered how Regan and Morrison were faring. Two damned crazy gringos, fight each other until both were bloody wrecks, then team up and run freight to a starving town, right through the middle of Apacheria, something de Cordova and his wagons would not do. He had a hunch that Juan de Cordova had lost much face due to his turning down the Mogollon freight, and face, to de Cordova, meant everything.

He was sure de Cordova was aware of this. Now, he waited patiently, slumped in his chair, trying to guess how de Cordova would attempt to regain that face. He did not have long to wait.

For the talk switched to the amount of grub in the town. Shut off from the world, how much food was left in stores. Valenzuela, owning the only real big store, would be the authority on that. He judged he had about a week's supply left.

Cortinas noticed that Juan de Cordova listened carefully, adding no words until the discussion was over. Then de Cordova cleared his throat, hammered softly with the ink bottle he used as a gavel.

"You talk as though Silver City will be an island, miles from anywhere, marooned to starve to death on an island mountain. This is not true, gentlemen. I assure you—from the bottom of my heart —that New Mexico Wagons will keep a freight line between here and El Paso, even if we die to the last man to keep it open."

He looked at one mine owner, the one who'd said, "What good is gold or silver, if you can't get it out to market?"

He's had his little hunk of revenge, Cortinas thought.

"You going to freight out gold and silver, too?" Cortinas asked, rubbing salt on the wound.

"Commerce will go on as usual," Juan de Cordova said quietly.

Cortinas thought, He's not so stupid. He knows that if he doesn't haul freight, Jim Regan will, if Regan gets back. And that damn' Irishman might just come back. He's that kind.

The subject of martial law came up. Governor Lew Wallace would have to proclaim it, though, and Governor Wallace knew nothing about this country and its demands and dangers—hell, he was sitting on his fat butt down safe in Old Mesilla, a political appointee, writing a book. There was no wire out since abandonment of Fort Bayard. Apaches had cut the wire in thousands of pieces. Apaches thought each dot or dash lay in a certain length of wire. Therefore, they had cut it into short lengths to cut out the dots and dashes.

There'd be no use sending runners out north to Fort Defiance or Fort Apache. Both had their hands full of Apaches. The same was true of Fort Davis, down in Texas, about two hundred miles southeast of El Paso. Colonel Grierson there, according to rumor, had already tangled with Victorio, losing six out of his Tenth Cavalry scouting party. Victorio had the entire Apache nation on the move with rifles, pistols, and war-axes. And Fort Staunton. . . . Victorio had escaped from Fort Staunton, so there was no use appealing to the general there. Silver City indeed was an island of abandonment.

Victorio himself, the filthy savage, the killing marauder, was supposed to be down in Old Mexico now, whipping the rurales at every turn, enlisting the aid of the Yaquis. And the Comanches, over on the Plains, were moving, too—Fort Davis and Colonel Grierson had their hands full of hell, what with comanches raiding on the east and north, with the Big Bend trampled by Yaqui and Apache war-parties. Maybe Silver City was luckier than Fort Davis and the Davis Mountains. They had only Apache to fight. And in this grim bit of reality they seemed to find a strange source of solace. Misery loves company, Cortinas thought idly.

Where did their hope then lie? Not in the army, for the army had its hands full, not only in this Territory, but also in the State of Texas and over west in Arizona Territory.

They fell then to cursing the United States government, a popular pastime, even then in this year of 1879, and especially they swore at a branch of that government, the United States Army. They had been much better under the Mexican government, somebody stated hotly. At least the Mexican government recognised the Yaquis, Comanches, Apaches, as genuinely serious enemies, not as predatory minor raiders out on some mystic place called, for lack of a better name, The Frontier.

Cortinas did not agree with this, but said nothing. He knew that the US army policy, in many phases, was not adequate, but he also knew that the army could not attract good soldiers, only the riffraff that could not place itself socially and economically after the Civil War. Army pay was very low. Desertions and deflections were many.

The discussion got very angry. It lost

perspective and they became men railing against their government and fate.

Cortinas got to his feet. "I move the meeting be adjourned."

They were so upset and hot, nobody took cognisance of the fact he was not even a member of the town council, but the motion was seconded and passed, and they filed out talking to each other.

They split into twos and threes and left, apparently going to their homes, but Cortinas knew this was only a blind—they would almost all wind up at the bar in Madame Beauvrais' sporting house. Some of these men, he knew, had two families—one here in Silver City and another in Mexico City or Guadalajara or somewhere in Mexico. Some even had a common-law wife and children somewhere in the cabbes of Silver City. In Cortinas' viewpoint there were few women as pretty as these young Mexican peon girls, with their full breasts, their thin waists and rather wide hips. He did not blame them. Had he enough money he'd probably have two wives, too.

It was a warm fall evening. Later on, about midnight, the winter chill would creep down from the northern Pinos Altos, by morning lawns would be covered with fine white frost. A sickle of a moon rode a cloudless sky. The mills made their usual whining noise.

Cortinas became aware of Juan de Cordova standing beside him. He had a momentary touch of dislike for this tall, hard man with the cruel mouth, the hawked nose, the icy eyes. He knew that de Cordova did not especially care for him. De Cordova did not dislike him; he merely mistrusted him. Cortinas thought with wry humor, He can't get me under his thumb, and that bothers him.

"Cigar, Joseph."

Cortinas said thanks, lit the cigar, and inhaled deeply. Finest Habana cigar made. Juan de Cordova didn't give away his best cigar without a point in mind. Cortinas decided to beat him to the bag.

"Wonder how Regan and Morrison are faring?"

He heard de Cordova inhale deeply.

156

Finally de Cordova said, "I don't know whether they're brave or stupid, or just showing off."

"Three days," Joseph Cortinas said. "They should be up around the Gila by now, probably beyond it."

"If they're alive."

Again, a touch of inner mirth was in the newspaper man. He got the thought that he and de Cordova were two inquisitive dogs, circling the other to see what he had. Cortinas decided to see if de Cordova would show his fangs. "Think they'll make it there and back?"

"How would I know?"

Cortinas shrugged, looked at his cigar's coal. "You've been over that trail many, many times. I just asked your opinion."

De Cordova was silent for a long moment. Then he said, "Last time we freighted it the Apaches weren't hitting like they are now. What did you think of the meeting? Got sort of hot there for a while."

Now he's asking my opinion. He's after

something. He thinks he's got his long nose under my tail.

"The boys got a chance to blow off steam."

"Nothing more?"

"I think it was a good move to hire Gonzales. If anybody knows how to slaughter a fellow humanely, the General is your man. He did all right murdering Maximilian's peons."

"You're cynical."

"Born that way, I guess."

"It's either kill or be killed. Those Chiricahuas under Geronimo are burning and murdering in Arizona. Hitting ranches and mines. There's even talk they might raid Tucson. These Apaches are all united now—Victorio handling things here, Geronimo in Mexico and Arizona. And you say they're not dangerous?"

"I didn't say that." Cortinas had gained his objective. He smiled quietly in the dark. "Don't tromp me down with those high-heeled Spanish boots, Juan. If this town falls, you're not the only one to get his hair lifted. I've got a wife and children; you haven't. But one point you're thinking of sort of amuses me in a macabre way."

"And that?"

"You all talked as though the Apaches were grouped outside of Silver City right now, getting ready to attack. This town has a lot of rifles. This is a pretty big town to hit."

Their cigars glowed. This town pulsed, moved, stood still, saw sin, saw glory. And out in the mountains Apaches roamed.

Cortinas asked, "Haven't lost a wagon so far, have you?"

"No."

"Only one who's lost wagons is Regan, then."

There the name was again. Regan. Jim Regan.

"And if Ramosa had sent those wagons over the Espejo instead of the Mimbres, I doubt if Apaches would have hit them."

Suddenly Juan de Cordova threw away his cigar. It spun into the street and landed with scattering sparks. Cortinas saw it had been smoked less than half.

"Good night, Cortinas."

"Good night, Juan."

Juan de Cordova walked across the street, turned down half a block, and entered the compound of New Mexico Wagons. His polished boots ground on gravel. He got the smell of hay and mules and manure. A huge lantern hung over the centre of the compound on cables strung in from the buildings. The place was quiet—the blacksmith's forge was cold, mules munched hay in stalls. The night watchman and his flunky had mules harnessed for the stage trip to El Paso. Juan de Cordova dug out his big watch.

"Stage is over half an hour late," he said.

"About that," the watchman said.

The flunky said nothing, standing with his hat in his hand. He always took off his old hat when de Cordova came around. It irritated de Cordova on this night; usually, it pleased him.

He saw a light in the back door's panel.

Maria was staring out the front window and she turned quickly, lamplight glowing on her red hair.

"What are you doing here at this hour?"

"I had to finish some book-keeping. The stage is very late, Juan."

"I know it."

"You don't suppose—"

"No, I don't *suppose*." His voice was a little too harsh. "There might have been a flash flood down around Carrizo or some other wash. There were thick clouds over the desert this afternoon."

"I hope you're right."

He did not look at his sister. He looked down at some papers on his desk, but his mind was not on their contents. There was something missing here, something about her he couldn't understand—try hard as he did to put a finger on it. Somehow, it seemed to revolve around her and Regan, but he knew this was only fanciful thinking on his part. Or was it?

"You had better go home," he said

slowly. "The flunky will drive you home. You can't work all the time, you know."

"When I work I don't have time to worry."

"Worry never solved a problem in the world."

She took her *rebozo* and wrapped it over her slender shoulders. The many colors of the Mexican-made shawl still made her hair seem redder. She was small and beautiful, with her pert nose, her saucy eyes, her full lips. He thought suddenly, The man who gets her to wife will get the world's best. And by God, if he doesn't treat her right, he'll have me to account to! He smiled at that thought.

She paused at the back door. "I've heard the men talk. They want more money. They claim they'll have to get more money or they won't freight through Apache rifles and arrows."

"I've been expecting that. I'll call a meeting tomorrow."

"Why don't you come home with me?"

"I have some business to attend to."

She hesitated momentarily, then words

broke from her. "Business! With *Madame* Beauvrais—in her house of fallen women! Oh, God in heaven, a de Cordova, running a house of ill fame! Oh, God, I'm glad mother and father are dead—!"

Face stern, he lunged for her, but she danced out of reach, face high with color. She ran out the door, slamming it behind her. He made no move to follow her. He stood there, face cold and blank. She'd never acted this way before.

Was it because of this Apache terror? Yes, some of it could be blamed on that, he was sure. Yes, and this Regan—and the trouble he personified. Blood hammered in his veins. Soon he heard buggy wheels grate on gravel as the rig left the compound.

Only then did he move.

He went out the back door and crossed the compound to the bunk-house. He walked down the aisle between the bunks. The air was close, twenty odd men slept here, they snored, there was the stink of unwashed bodies. He found the man he wanted on the end bunk.

For a moment he stood and looked down at him. He saw a huge, bloated face, veins broken into red lines by drink, thick lips and a wide nose. He shook the man gently. Bulging eyes opened slowly, regarding him in the dim lamplight. Juan de Cordova squatted, lips to the man's ear.

"You know Regan?"

"Yeah, when I see him."

"He and Morrison pulled out freight for Mogollon. You know that, don't you?"

"Everybody knows that."

"They might come back," de Cordova said meaningly.

Heavy eyes moved in damp sockets. "They might not, too. I get what you mean, boss."

"Scouts have brought word in, that Apaches have burned Santa Margarita *rancho*. A man could hide behind one of those adobe walls with a rifle."

"Should I take somebody with me?"

"No, go alone. You're the only one I can trust, Charlie." You lie to boost the ego of an ignorant man. "Scalp them, burn their wagons. Kill their mules. Make it look like Apaches."

"How much?"

"Two hundred *pesos*. One hundred now, the other hundred when I see scalps."

"When do I leave?"

"Right now."

Charlie Parks hurriedly dressed and met him outside. De Cordova paid him and left. He went up Bullard and then turned west; soon he was on the outskirts of town.

A huge two-story house loomed ahead, surrounded by a high stone wall. He walked through the high archway into a beautiful garden. This had been the family home of the Villalobos who, for centuries had made millions out of Santa Rita copper. For centuries convict labor sent up from Mexico City had worked the open pits.

With the War over, copper had sunk to new low depths. No more convict labor toiled upward from Mexico City. US peons refused to work for a peso a day.

Five years ago the Villalobos had deserted this huge mansion. For three years it had been unoccupied.

He'd bought the house at a bargain, dealing with the Villalobos who were now in Mexico, where the family also had huge holdings. Madame Beauvrais ran it for him. She had a sharp brain, was a good manager—and she had a warm, curvaceous body.

She reserved her body just for him.

Suddenly he remembered Maria's bitter words. He tried to brush them aside. He could not do this.

His mind dwelt momentarily on a rumor he'd heard regarding Santa Rita Copper Pits. This rumor said that the millionaire, Hearst, was negotiating for control of Santa Rita.

Hearst owned untold millions. He could buy Santa Rita as easily as he could snap his fingers. Hearst had made his fortune in silver in Virginia City, Nevada, and gold in Deadwood, South Dakota.

Hearst had run in rails . . . and had run Regan out. Soon the SP rails would reach Deming, sixty odd miles to the south. If Hearst bought Santa Rita, he might run in rails—a branch line to the copper. If he did this, New Mexico Wagons would be done. And so would Regan. That is, if Regan ever got a wagon to Silver City, got a wheel rolling.

Juan de Cordova had a cold feeling. The old order, he realised, was slowly changing. Once a man never heard English spoken in Silver City. Now more and more people were speaking English, not Spanish. The sons of the dons were going to lose, unless something was done soon. But what could one do?

Moonlight cast shadows through the flimsy branches of tall eucalyptus trees. The flagstone walk was loud under his boots. Shady live-oaks covered green patches of lawn with dark shadows. Roses bloomed and added their faint fine aroma to the stillness of the beautiful New Mexico night.

Suddenly he wanted the madame. He

wanted to feel her soft body, see her eyes move across his face, to reach into her and feel her, and become satisfied—at least, for the moment.

He entered by the back door.

He walked down an arched walkway floored with granite. Ahead was an enormous high-domed room. Villalobos had allowed a lot of Moorish architecture to influence this huge home. A huge chandelier hung at the apex of the dome. Imported around the Horn from Lisbon, the rumor said. Forty tiny kerosene lamps, nestled in the glistening glass, lighted the room, with many chandeliers on the sides. The dome and walls were made of glistening blue and white mosaics.

Completely across the big room was another archway, similar to the one he now stood under; this was the front door. The long bar ran the entire length of the room, backbar behind it glistening with mirrors and bottles. The gaming tables and roulette wheels occupied the rest of the room.

There were no shoddy, boisterous Irish miners in here. They were not admitted. Here was allowed only the cream and wealth of Silver City. Mine-owners, mine superintendents, merchants, and others of good income. No overalls, blue chambray shirts, or scuffed boots here. Carefully-tailored suits, cutaway coats, ties and white shirts, highly polished boots, bench made.

He ran his eye over the bar, noticing it was not well filled. They seemed to be interested in a game running at a far table, a poker table. Men and women crowded around—he saw bare shoulders, heard the squeals of women, saw the dance of light in carefully coiffeured hair.

Madame has some new girls, he thought. They must have come in on the morning stage. He had been busy talking to the driver back by the barn.

Apparently nobody noticed him.

He turned to his right, slowly climbing the stairway leading to the second floor. The red carpeting was rich and springy under his boots. He came to a widow's walk that ran entirely around the room. Off it were doors into the cribs. The walk gained, he looked over the iron railing at the crowd below.

All the members of the town council, with the exception of Lamas and Cortinas, were here, he noticed.

He saw a man and woman come out of a door at the end of the walk. He recognised the engineer, John Watson, and one of the girls. He did not know the girl—she was a new one. He looked at them with casual interest. He thought, John hasn't compromised Maria yet, or else he wouldn't be rolling with a whore in a crib. Or had he? Hard to tell about your fellow men. . . .

He entered a room. Madame Beauvrais' room was never locked. The room was thick with her smell—the eternal smell of women, of perfume, of clothing. The furniture was of heavy oak—a matched set left by the Villalobos—hand-carved and old. A crocheted bedspread covered the huge oaken bed. He crossed the room and opened the french windows.

From this high vantage he could look down on Silver City. He saw Bullard Street—the main street—with its business houses. Few of the peon lights in the adobes were glowing—they went to bed with the sun, awakened with the sun. He could not see the de Cordova mansion from here. It was on the east side across town.

He remembered his talk with Joseph Cortinas.

Cortinas had printed a one page extra when Fort Bayard had been abandoned. Half of the page was concerned with Jim Regan. Regan, who was risking his life, and the life of Frank Morrison, by breaking through Apacheria to save starving Mogollon.

He knew what people were thinking. New Mexico Wagons for years had hauled all supplies into Mogollon. Now two strangers were on the move. Why weren't New Mexico Wagons hauling these provisions? Was New Mexico Wagons—and Juan de Cordova—yellow?

Regan, damn you.

His mood changed when he heard the door behind him open, then softly close. He did not look around. He felt a small hand slide into his. Only then did he look down. Her glistening coal black hair came only to his breast.

"I didn't know you'd come, lover. Then I talked to a girl downstairs. She told me about you coming."

That would be John Watson's girl of the night.

"What's the big attraction at the poker table?"

"Poker Alice Tubbs. She drifted in this afternoon. She's gambling with Morgan and I have two mules in the game."

"She winning?"

"I haven't checked. She just came down from the Black Hills."

His jaw muscles tightened. She realised she'd said the wrong thing: Black Hills. Jim Regan. Black Hills. She tightened her grip on his hand. He looked down at her.

She was small, beautiful, compactly built. She wore a light blue strapless dress that revealed glistening white shoulders. Her breasts were large for her small body, giving her a touch of desired comeliness.

His mind flicked back to their first meeting. He'd been on vacation in New Orleans. They'd thrown a wild party in a house of ill fame. She'd been the madame. She said she was twenty six. He judged her thirty five.

They'd lain in bed and afterwards had talked. He liked the feel of her firm, curvaceous, compact little body. She wanted to run a bigger house, make more money. There was so much competition in New Orleans.

Suddenly he'd remembered the deserted Villalobo manor.

"Juan, you're so serious tonight."

Her brown eyes roved gently over his face. They were motherly and wise, humoring him, drawing him out. A tiny finger tiptoed up to touch his smooth shaven jaw. Slowly her hand went around his neck. She stood on tiptoe, arched

173

against him, hips moving slightly, as they kissed long and ardently.

They broke and she smiled at him.

"Juan, what is wrong with the stage?"

Again—the stage! Why had she asked that. "Nothing, I guess. Just a little late, that's all."

"Three of the new girls missed the morning stage in El Paso, and are coming out on the evening stage, the other girls told me." Suddenly her voice became frightened. "Juan, what *are* you staring at?"

"Look!"

She whirled and looked out the window but she watched the town below, not the desert beyond. "I see nothing wrong."

"Out on the desert."

She saw it, then, a tongue of fire in the night; it might have been ten miles away, or forty. The desert is deceptive.

"Apaches are burning the stage!"

He had no reply.

She gave him an upward glance. He stared at the distant flames, thin face hard cold, jaw carved from granite. Next morning at daybreak, face still craggy and dead, he rode south, ahead of his lumbering freight-wagons, tall and deadly and silent, Sharps across the fork of his Chihuahua saddle.

9

AFTER fording the Gila River, Regan and Morrison made better time, for the foothills were behind them and they were on the edge of the desert—tiny ants inching across the blazing inferno. They found the San Francisco River and, true to Morrison's predictions, the water was low. The road zigzagged, fording the river many times, but the crossings had gravel bottoms, and that made it easier on wagons, mules and men.

They did not camp on the San Francisco that night. The river was low with scant running water, and the water in potholes was green with scum, so they made camp below the Big Bend at Horse Springs, for here the water was clear, always running, and much cooler.

Also there was timber and brush along the San Francisco, and Horse Springs was more or less in the open, a bubbling desert spring with clear water—because of the low sagebrush surrounding Horse, a man would have a better chance to spot an Apache sneaking in.

Morrison took watch until twelve, but Regan could not sleep. He lay under the wagon, gazing up at the reach, and tried to kill his thoughts. Old Wad and Pedro and the mules. And he needed wagons and freight to haul. He saw the thin, hard face of Juan de Cordova. Yes, and the girlish face of Maria, saucy nose, inviting lips.

Morrison moved in, a black shadow in moonlight. He squatted. "Your turn, boss."

Regan crawled from under the wagon, rifle in hand. Morrison stood staunch against the night. "Too damn' calm."

"Let's hope it stays that way."

Morrison shook his shaggy head. "Too damned quiet."

Regan moved into the moonlight. He had no appetite for conversation. He checked the mules on picket-ropes. Sweet

Jasmine nibbled at his hand with grass-green teeth.

Regan batted the bony head aside.

The night passed slowly. Then the sun was on them, throwing steepled shadows across the western desert, the shadows moving back to the scarp mountains with the sun's advance. Morrison fried bacon and made sourdough biscuits and coffee. They hitched mules, and moved on again.

"Next stop," Morrison said, "is Mogollon. Damn, that little burg against that mountain will look good to me."

"How many hours?"

"Two o'clock this afternoon, I'd guess." Morrison paused. "Unless something happens."

Regan slapped him on the shoulder. "Cheerful cuss."

Mules slapped against collars, loosening heavy wheels. The grind began again, only this time the mules were pointed northeast into the mountains, instead of northwest into the desert. Here was upgrade climb all the way. And mules were tired. The men were tired.

Within a mile, they were entering San Francisco Canyon. At first the valley was about a mile wide, the river sluggish through the middle. It tapered to the northeast, this valley did, finally narrowing down to the defile that the river, tumbling for eons and eons, had carved through the granite mountains. Regan called halt.

"Let them blow for awhile."

They locked brakes and slack went the traces. Regan looked around him. The flat lands held scraggly chamiso, a few mesquite trees, and grey desert sage.

He mopped his forehead. "A man could sure build a nice ranch here."

Morrison glanced at him. "I thought your job was freighting?"

"Freighting will soon be gone. It'll be only a matter of a short time until the railroads will have it all." A man could run a dam across the river where it comes out of the canyon, build his main canals along the base of the hills, then run his laterals down toward the river.

"All this land needs is water."

Excitement stirred Regan. He could see the brush gone and the land levelled, the ditches filled with river water. Then this desert would be green with alfalfa and head-crops. Against the north wall a small mesa rose about twenty feet above the desert's floor. That would be the place to build the house and necessary barns and outbuildings.

"We'd better get moving," Morrison said. "First thing I know, you'll have a span of mules unhitched. You'll be ploughing with a wooden stick like they do down in Mexico."

Regan grinned. "Hit that collar, Sweet Jasmine."

Slowly the heavily-laden wagon started to move. Sweet Jasmine was getting old. Regan thought back and fixed her age at eleven. She'd been a colt when he'd bought her in Nuava Laredo from a Mexican mule-raiser.

The dusty road entered a narrow defile. On the right was the roaring San Francisco River. The river held more water here, but would lose it when it hit the sands below. They toiled through the canyon and entered another flat area, only about a hundred yards wide. Ahead was another narrow pass lined on each side by perpendicular rock cliffs.

They kept slowly moving on, the grade steadily climbing. Tension was in Regan, and his eyes scanned the stone walls. Morrison tied his lines to the brake handle, letting his team plod unguided, and walked beside him, rifle in hand. Regan glanced at him. Morrison's eyes missed nothing, moving over the lava walls, always moving.

Neither said much.

They made noon camp at a point where the walls spread out and made a small clearing. They left their wagons on the road and unhitched and turned mules loose to water and graze on the short grass along the bank. Each carried his rifle. He made sure his rifle was always in reach. Morrison warmed a can of beans over a small fire he'd made of dried driftwood. They ate nothing but beans. Regan lay on his back and looked at the cloudless New Mexico sky. Fatigue made him drowsy.

"What time will we hit Mogollon?"

"It's a tough uphill grade," Morrison said. "Our mules are damn' tired. I'd say about sundown."

"Narrow canyon all the way?"

"The canyon spreads out once more, about half a mile this side of Mogollon. They call it Rock Mesa."

Regan nodded.

They rested an hour. Then they re-hitched. Regan took the small box of dynamite out of his wagon where he'd placed it when they'd stopped at the gate of Williams' rancho.

He bound the box with rope to the reach under the wagon, Morrison doing likewise. Regan checked the detonator and fuse on three sticks of Morrison's dynamite, and nodded.

"You know how to handle it," he said.

They moved on again, wagon-wheels complaining on gravel. They forded the San Francisco, for the road crossed and recrossed the river. The fords were solidly made of gravel.

Neither man rode the high seats. They plodded beside their wagons, rifles in hand. After fording the river each shifted to the opposite side of his wagon. This way the bulk of the wagon was between each man and the menace of the cliffs.

Hot humid air filled the canyon. The only relief was fording the river. There the water was at least wet, if not cool. Four-thirty came and Morrison moved up even with him.

"About a mile ahead we leave the canyon. We come out on Rock Mesa. Mogollon is just around the bend."

Regan smiled. "Hell, maybe they let us through." Morrison shrugged and dropped back to his wagon.

It took twenty minutes by Regan's pocket-watch to make the grade. He walked beside Sweet Jasmine, feeling sorry for the laboring old mule. Then finally the road levelled and Rock Mesa was ahead.

Here the canyon widened to make a

valley about two hundred feet wide. Huge black igneous boulders reared heavy bulks out of the mesa floor. Sagebrush grew waist high, grey and scraggly. Beyond the boulders and the sagebrush rose the black granite cliffs, broken occasionally by diagonal ledges.

"About a mile from Mogollon," Morrison hollered. "She's right around that corner to the north, smack dab against the—"

He never finished his sentence. Suddenly Sweet Jasmine rose on her hind legs, squealing in gurgling pain. She came lurching down, landing in a heap. Then Regan heard the report of the rifle.

He saw a puff of smoke high on the wall of the north canyon. He did two things automatically: he locked the brakes on the wagon and ran under it, firing as he ran.

He heard the roar of Morrison's rifle. A hurried glance showed Morrison under his wagon, kneeling on one knee. Morrison shot toward a skirl of lazy powdersmoke that showed halfway up the jagged cliff.

Face cold, Regan put his rifle on that spot, and fired twice. Their deadly concentrated fire brought results.

The Apache uncoiled out of his hiding place on the ledge, a tawny brown figure wearing buckskin trousers and moccasins —a man of broken, torn body, fighting to pull air into his lungs. He poised that way for a long terrible minute, a thin red-streak slashed against the cream-white limestone of the cliff, and then his rifle fell, clattering down the slope. He followed it downward, lazily smashing against out-jutting boulders, finally to land in a sodden heap on the valley's floor.

"We got that bastard!" Morrison hollered.

Sweet Jasmine was attempting to struggle to her feet. A glance told Regan she had her forelegs under her. Her tough body shivered, she tried to push strength into her legs, but she couldn't make it, and she sank slowly back to the dust.

Mules were rearing, pawing the air. But brakes held them, and also the weight of Sweet Jasmine could not be moved. Regan saw that Morrison's off-lead mule was also down, blood coming from the hole in his head.

The Apaches had used their brains. Kill a lead mule and tie up the load, then pick off the skinners. A bullet tore into the gravel ahead of him, sending back stinging bits of sharp stone into his face.

The fight was tough, fierce, savage—and did not last long. It could not last too long, Regan realised; if it did, he and Morrison would be doomed. He doubted if the sharp sounds of rifles could reach around the scarp wall ahead and echo into Mogollon. It was himself and Morrison, with no outside chance of bringing in extra rifles.

A bullet hit a wagon-spoke to his right. It sent dried slivers flying, leaving a grey jagged hole in the spoke. Regan had glimpsed the Apache rise hurriedly, rifle to his shoulder, then duck back down into the boulders ahead, about thirty or forty feet.

Regan said, "They're concentrated in that bunch of sand rock ahead. They had that one on the cliff to shoot down mules."

"No more on the cliff," Morrison yelled in return. Regan cursed with dull monotony. Ahead of him was a dense wall of boulders and thick grey sagebrush. He took a chance, raised his head, looked around—the bullet came out of the pile of boulders, smashing into the wagon beside his head. His head came down.

He had glimpsed the Apache, but had not had time to shoot in return. The warrior had suddenly risen out of the boulders, rifle to his shoulder; he'd shot, then ducked quickly out of sight.

Regan thought, They're using rifles and not arrows. The arrows, he figured, would come later . . . if they came. Fire arrows, sliding out of the protection of the boulders, flame spewing behind them, then lodging in their wagons.

Regan hollered, "Black powder, Morrison."

Morrison slanted him an evil, whiskery smile. Despite his heavy beard, the scar on his cheek stood out with red lividness.

"Holler when, boss!"

Regan reached into the box of dynamite. He had the cap already fastened, all he needed was to light the fuse. His hands trembled as he found matches in his pocket. He glanced at Morrison. Morrison was ahead of him, waiting, dynamite in one hand, the cap on, match ready.

"Heave it way out," Regan ordered. "They're in those boulders. You throw for the south end of the rocks, I'll take the north. But way out, man—or else we'll go up with it."

Something trickled out of the wagon and dropped on Regan's neck. He ran a hand up and saw it was brown in color. A bullet had ploughed through a carton of pork and beans. The sauce was dripping out.

Fumblingly, he lit a match, applied it

to the fuse. The match flickered, almost died, then gained strength; the fuse caught fire. It burned with a sparkling rapidity.

Regan leaped to his feet, hollered, "Now, Morrison," and ran forward. He hurled the dynamite the way a man hurls a javelin. Every ounce of his wiry body, every bit of strength he owned, went behind the heave. From the corner of his eye he saw Morrison repeating his performance. Morrison's face was savage, his body hunched.

Then the dynamite left Regan's hand. It arced in the air, lazy and tumbling end over end, the sparks spitting from the fuse. Regan saw it land in the boulders, bounce off one, then drop out of sight.

Quickly he threw himself on the ground. A glance told him Morrison was also prone on his belly. There was a short and ugly pause—a dull moment of silence —and then the roars lifted the earth, smashed the boulders aside, hammered against Regan's eardrums, shaking the ground under him.

Boulders spewed upward as though expelled by an angry volcano. Dust shot up, hiding the scene. One boulder went higher than the others, smashing against the blue of the sky. Behind it, trailing it, came the body of an Apache, drifting upward. A leg fell off, an arm twisted and went to one side. The boulder reached the apex of its lift, hesitated momentarily.

The Apache hesitated, too. Suddenly the body went into small fragments, and there was only his head, floating below the boulder. Then the head and boulder toppled to the ground.

A rock slammed into the wagon box, fell to the ground. Another hit Regan on the back just below his shoulders. The sudden pain ran through him, and his breath came in jerky wheezes. Ahead was dense yellow desert dust. He got to his feet, back hurting.

"There goes one!"

Morrison's yell held triumph. Regan saw him run forward, go suddenly to one knee, then fire. He got a glimpse of the fleeing Apache over the sagebrush, and then the Apache sank from sight.

Morrison said, "Another two hundred and fifty bucks!"

By now Regan was on his feet. Morrison came over to him, face grave with anxiety.

"You get hit, Boss?"

"Boulder hit me."

Morrison held his rifle ready, scanning the sagebrush. The mules had stopped fighting now, and there was no alien sound. Nothing moved out in the brush. The dynamite had torn the nest of boulders apart. It had split the sandstone rocks, smashing some of them into bits.

"They must've been all holed up in those boulders," Regan said.

Morrison asked, "Did you see that one come apart?"

Regan remembered the dusky body rising, the legs and arms peeling off, then the explosion within the body, and the head poising over the edge of the world, looking at the world—a head without a body.

"I've never seen anything like it in my life," he truthfully said, "and I never want to see it again, either."

"It wasn't pretty."

Regan said, "Circle through the brush. There might be one laying out just wounded."

They parted going into the brush. Regan walked slowly, eyes missing nothing. He saw a leg, broken and scorched, and came across the torso of the redskin, burned and seared. He met Morrison on the other side of the boulder patch. Morrison shrugged. "Nothing."

"You look around in the boulders. I'll get the one that we knocked off the cliff."

Morrison said "Scalp him. Two hundred and fifty bucks, you know."

Regan shook his head.

He found the Apache in the rocks, lying wedged between two granite boulders. He found the Apache's rifle. The fall had broken the stock, but the rifle barrel seemed all right. He found three bullets in the Apache. He lifted the broken, limp body over his shoulder and carried it back to the wagon, where he dumped it on the ground.

He squatted there, smoking a cigarette, hands trembling. He could hear Morrison moving in the brush. Regan had to move, so he went to Sweet Jasmine. The mule was dead. She lay on her side, eyes extended, mouth open, deer flies already gathered around her blood.

He was standing there when Morrison came up carrying five bloody scalps. Morrison had used no finesse in his scalping. He had skinned off the entire scalp. His hands were bloody.

He threw the gory scalps on his wagon-seat. "You find the head?" he asked.

Regan shook his head.

"Two hundred and fifty bucks in that head." Morrison glanced at the Apache Regan had toted in. "I'll handle him later." His eyes met Regan's. "I wonder if anybody got away?"

"There could have been a few others. That dynamite might have scared the living hell out of them. Superstitious as they are, they probably thought it was the Menitou sending lightning at them."

Morrison said, "Thought I saw one dive over the river bank, but I never got a shot at him. Anyway, if I did see one, he's long gone from now. What a story he'll tell Victorio." He chuckled.

Morrison went back into the rocks. Regan unhitched Sweet Jasmine. He unhitched the other lead mule, tied a rope around Jasmine's neck, and dragged her carcass from the road into the brush. He did the same with Morrison's dead mule.

Morrison came out of the brush, grinning like a devil. He carried a head by the hair.

"Damn it, Regan, he looks familiar to me."

Regan looked at the powder-burned, ugly head. The forehead was wide and low, the cheekbones high, the nose broad, the lips full and the mouth wide. You could have seen this face alive, on top of broad shoulders, and its ugliness would never be forgotten, Regan realised. Now dead and independent of the shoulders, it seemed the ugliest thing on earth.

"He's homely enough," Regan said.

Morrison tossed the head up on his wagon's seat, there it landed beside the scalps with a dull thud. He went to his knees, knife in hand, and started to scalp the remaining Apache.

Regan said, "I'm going to lace the wagons together."

"Soon as I lift this hair I'll be with you."

Regan unhooked Morrison's mules and led them to one side. He let his wagon coast back until it was two feet from the front end of the box on Morrison's wagon, then with chain he lashed its tongue to the reach of the first wagon. He ran the chain back to the sprocket of the second wagon. Then he hitched Morrison's mules onto the first wagon, making a team of three spans.

Morrison was out in the brush, looking for more scalps. Regan remembered reading somewhere that present-day man was removed only four hundred generations from the Neanderthal Man, that flat browed, hairy and shaggy man of low intelligence, who scented the wind like a wild animal, beady eyes glowing. Morrison seemed to have leaped back those four hundred generations in one small jump. He prowled the torn rocks and brush, eyes on the ground, hunger in his heart.

Regan called sharply. "Come on, let's move."

Morrison jerked up his head. "All right," he said slowly.

The mules seemed anxious to leave this spot of death. They dug in, lying low against collars, hoofs digging to get the heavy load started. Regan put his shoulder to the wagon, and Morrison did likewise. Slowly the two heavy wagons started to roll, wheels crunching gravel. A mule slipped, went to his knees, scrambled upright, dug in again.

The work was slow and back-breaking. Mules pulled, nostrils wide, sucking in air, and men pushed, boots sliding on shale. It seemed ages to Regan until they rounded the corner of the cliff. Ahead lay a steep grade, winding along the north flank of the mountain, a narrow trail carved into igneous rock.

"Mogollon is around that bend," Morrison shouted. "You can't see it from here."

Slowly, with agonised grunts from mules and men, they conquered the grade, not daring to stop, for they did not own the combined energy to get the loads moving again, once they halted on this grade.

They inched up the grade. The sun was terribly hot, scorching the silent earth, sucking up its last vestige of moisture. Scrub cedar filled the air with strong perfume. Below, the river twisted through rocks, a thin sickly stream. Regan's boots slipped, and he went to his knees.

"Saying your prayers?" Morrison joked, shoulder to the wagon box, pushing with all his weight, face bathed with sweat.

Regan got to his feet. He cupped his

hands to his mouth. "We need help," he hollered. "Loads coming up the grade, people. Supplies, grub. Come and help."

The words echoed from one stone cliff to the other. They rolled and tumbled across space, dying finally in the sun-blasted heat.

"One of us could go ahead," Morrison said, "and get help. There might be a mule or two in Mogollon."

"Williams said they'd eaten them."

"I doubt if your words reached town," Morrison said.

At last, the summit was reached. Ahead was a wide alluvial cone that lay along the base of the cliff. Endless waters across endless eons had washed the cone down. On this, men had built Mogollon. Ahead, a quarter mile, were sun-beaten shacks, some of frame lumber, some of logs, but most made of adobe.

They were on level ground now. Mules staggered forward, slobber hanging in dirty ropes from gaping jaws. Wagon wheels smashed gravel. Regan thought, Maybe everybody is dead, for nobody apparently saw them. Then the thought came that, had Apaches sacked the dirty, ugly town, they would have burned it.

They were almost to the first buildings when somebody hollered, "Hey, what the hell is this?" and a man came out of an adobe shack. He was a tall, middle-aged man wearing only dirty trousers. Behind him crowded a fat Mexican woman, rigged by the proverbial *ninos* and *ninas* who stared with brown liquid eyes, all attempting to hang onto the mother's wide dress.

The town, such as it was, came alive then. Men and women pushed, eyes glowing, and they coasted into town, stopping in front of the General Store, a weather-beaten log building.

Children ran hollering and playing. Adults pounded each other, hammered on Regan and Morrison, and yelled like idiots. Morrison scooped up two little girls, boosted one on each shoulder, and did a war-dance, the girls screaming and laughing.

The store-keeper, a heavy-set middle-aged man, said, "You boys sit on the bench. Jaime, bring them some beer. There's some cold bottles—just two of them—hanging in the well. I've saved them for this."

Regan sank onto the bench in the shade of the porch. Hands were unloading the wagons, carrying merchandise into the store. A Mexican boy came rushing up with two bottles of foaming beer. He gave them each a bottle, hesitated, then stopped, and embraced both, kissing each on the forehead. Suddenly he seemed ashamed of his display of emotion and scooted into the store.

Morrison said, "Me, a damn' hero. This is good beer."

"It's at least wet," Regan said.

The *jefe*—the mayor—talked to them. He had a big belly and stove-pipe thin legs. No, Senor Williams had not shown up. Nobody had seen him since they'd given him the money to take to Silver City. The people in the town had resigned themselves to die of starvation. This was manna from heaven.

One point, the *jefe* said, had bothered his people very much. Father Valenzuela had died two days ago, apparently of starvation. There would have been no Man of God to give final sacraments.

Regan told briefly of the fight on the mesa. The roar of the dynamite had not reached Mogollon. The *jefe* sent three men down to skin out Sweet Jasmine and the other mule. "We need the meat," he explained simply.

Regan smiled. "Sweet Jasmine will make tough chewing."

The *jefe* wanted to buy their mules for meat; Regan finally consented. He and Morrison would hike back across the canyons. That would be the safer route; Apaches would watch the wagon road.

Morrison killed his beer. He got a sack and put his scalps in it. A crowd grouped around him. A boy of about ten carried the Apache head over to Regan.

"I know who this is," he said proudly.

"Who?"

"Cabazon."

Cabazon in Spanish meant *he of the*

ugly head. The Apache had been correctly named.

"Victorio'll be out to kill you two now," the boy said. "More than ever since you killed Cabazon."

"Why?"

"Victorio and Cabazon are blood brothers."

10

THEY left Mogollon before dawn. The early morning of the fourth day found them staggering down the canyon, past the dam, and onto the alfalfa field, where Old Wad was irrigating.

"You never made it, eh?"

Morrison answered with, "To hell we didn't!"

They started toward the house. "Things have changed," Old Wad said. "Williams don't own this land any more."

Regan's bloodshot eyes studied him. "Who does?"

"That judge friend of de Cordova declared Williams insane. He claims the territory now owns this land. The judge made Juan de Cordova administrator of this land. De Cordova says we got to move."

"The hell we will move," Regan said.

"The judge and de Cordova was out here last night. They gave me until tonight to get out."

"That was nice of them," Regan said.

Old Wad sniffed the air. "What in the name of hell is that awful stink? Comes from that sack you tote, Morrison."

"Scalps." Morrison grinned, "Seventeen hundred and fifty bucks worth of stink, old timer."

They told Old Wad about the trip. Now they were closer to the house and Regan saw children playing in the yard.

"Whose kids are those?"

"We got a family since you left," Old Wad said. "Guy named Reynolds and his tribe. Apaches drove him off Agua Fria Springs. Came in three days ago and said he'd met you and he figured it was all right to camp here, so I let him stay."

"His family get through all right?" Morrison asked.

"They lost one kid. Oldest girl. Named Conchita."

Regan had a momentary remembrance

of Conchita: her womanly figure, mature and ripe, her brown beautiful eyes.

"Apaches capture her?" Morrison's voice was hoarse.

Old Wad shook his head. "She got wounded. She died during the night. Her pappy buried her."

Regan glanced at Morrison, whose face was granite. "Better that way," Morrison finally said.

There had been no raids. The mules were okay and picking up flesh fast, because the alfalfa was responding immediately to irrigation. Old Reynolds and his brood came out to meet them, the children running and shouting. The terrier, Constantinople, barked and frisked through the children, and Regan thought, I never expected a welcome like this.

Pedro was irrigating at the far end of the rancho and he came in to hear all the news.

Regan stumbled into the coolness of the house, finding a chair. The Senora Reynolds hurried with cool water from the well. Morrison and Reynolds remained outside, looking at Morrison's scalps and the head of Cabazon.

Regan heard Reynolds say, "They'll pay you five hundred for Cabazon. He's on the pink list."

Morrison came in and they ate. Utter fatigue was in both Regan and Morrison, for there had been little sleep—only catnaps behind boulders, one man always on guard. After eating, Regan went to sleep in the chair, but noon found him riding into Silver City, Old Wad riding with him—Morrison still slept back at the *rancho*.

Old Wad carried the sack holding the head and scalps. "Morrison wanted me to collect for them."

"Even the dogs are following us," Regan said.

Regan had expected people to come out and gather around them, although the noon sun was boiling hot. But nobody came. Town residents clung to the west side of Bullard Avenue, the shady side.

Cortinas came to the door of his shop

wearing a leather apron. "See you made it," he said. "Got a moment? I want to get your story."

"In a little while," Regan said.

He and Morrison had accomplished the impossible. But apparently it made no difference to this town. Now, for the first time, he really saw the hold the de Cordova's had over Silver City.

Old Wad said, "I'm going over to the bank and collect Morrison's money." His seamed eyes searched Regan's face. "Where you going?"

"See Juan de Cordova."

"Maybe I'd better go with you?"

Regan smiled. "You go to the bank"

Nobody sat on the bench in front of New Mexico Wagons office. Regan went inside. Maria de Cordova sat behind her desk doing some book-keeping.

"Well," she said, "I see you made it." She hesitated. "How about Morrison?"

"He came back, too. Your brother around?"

Her dark eyes watched him silently for a moment.

She was beautiful and cold, not the woman who'd hurriedly kissed him in the alley, over a week ago.

"No."

"Where is he?"

Her voice held no warmth. "That's none of your business, but I'll tell you anyway. He's riding rifle on the stage that left a few hours ago."

"You've had trouble?"

She told about Apaches jumping the stage. "They killed everybody on it. Right after you and Morrison left."

"They haven't hit your wagon trains, I take it?"

She shook her head. Facets of light danced from her red hair. Regan admired the pretty nose, the smooth cheek, her inviting mouth. His heart beat heavier.

She lifted her eyes. "No, not so far. But Juan has guards going out with each train and each stage."

Their eyes met. Their eyes held. Regan saw a faint blush touch her cheeks, she lowered her head to her ledger, and the blush went over her face, making her look girlish and even more lovely.

"Where does the judge live?" Regan asked.

She didn't look up. "I asked Juan not to go through with that silly insanity report, he's as bullheaded as father was." She told him where the judge lived. Suddenly she looked squarely at him again, the blush gone, her eyes steady. "Mr. Regan, why don't you give up and move out of Silver City?"

Regan's eyes were serious. "I can't do that," he said slowly. "I won't do it, either."

"Pride?"

"You can call it that, Miss de Cordova, if you wish. But maybe pride isn't all of it, you know. A man has to land somewhere and settle down. He can't be a wagon bum all his life, you know."

"There are other places to settle."

"No place where there is much freighting, though," he corrected. "Silver City is the last big freight center left in the West."

"You stay here," she said, "and you know what will happen, don't you?"

Regan nodded.

"Look," she said suddenly. "I'm sorry I kissed you back in that alley. It was a rash, impulsive act, and now I'm sorry I did it."

"I wonder," Regan murmured, and left.

Judge Alberto Gonzales lived a block off Bullard in a huge rambling adobe house. A trim Mexican maid admitted Regan to the judge's study. The judge sat like a huge toad behind an ornate desk. He did not get to his feet to shake hands.

"Your name is Regan, isn't it?"

"It is. I've got something for you, judge."

Slowly Regan tore the court order to small pieces. Judge Gonzales watched him with eyes that were not too steady. Regan threw the pieces into the judge's face. They trickled over his massive blue-shaven face like heavy snowflakes.

"That's what I think of you and your court order," Regan said thickly. "You or one of Garcia's deputies or de Cordova set foot on the Williams' *rancho* again I kill you. And if I don't, one of my men will —under my orders."

The jurist wet his fat lips. "You can't get by with it," he said in Spanish.

"Try me," Regan said, also in Spanish.

"You've got a lot to learn, *Senor* Regan. Silver City belongs to us Mexicans."

"I've heard that before, too. Just keep off the Williams' *rancho.*"

Judge Alberto Gonzales again wet his lips, but said nothing. Regan realised there was no physical menace in this bloated *politico*. This man would fight underground, letting others do his physical work.

Regan left.

Downtown, Old Wad was counting Morrison's money and swearing at the banker Lamas. "He tried to pay me only two fifty for Cabazon's head," he said. "Dirty damn' gyp."

"What did you get?"

"Five hundred."

"How?"

Old Wad tapped his gun handle.

Across the street was a wide board on the front of a building. Here two men were mounting Cabazon's ugly head onto a huge spike. A crowd had gathered around to watch. The men jammed the head on the spike and stood beside their ladders appraising their work. Cabazon's head had shrunken much since death. It did not look so big and gruesome now. They'd wired back the corners of the mouth to give the skull a fierce scowl.

"You look for the mail?" Regan asked.

"Haven't had time."

Regan realised he had not heard from Ramosa, wagon maker in El Paso de Norte, which seemed odd. He went to the post-office. He had only one letter and it was from Ramosa. He knew its contents before tearing it open.

Ramosa had the wagons built. He would not deliver them. Word had got back to him that the first three wagons had been burned by Mimbres Apaches, the drivers murdered, the mules butchered. If you want your wagons, come after them.

What good were wagons without freight to haul? He went to Cortinas' office. Cortinas was sitting behind his old desk, doing some writing. He swung around in his swivel chair with a smile on his thin, handsome face.

"So the hero has come home. And the hero found nothing has changed, despite his bravery. Now tell me about your trip?"

"Shoot the questions. Every time I get my name in your paper it's good advertising. Run my ad again next issue, too."

Regan answered the questions automatically, mind far away on other things. Next door to Cortinas' shop was an empty building. Finally he rudely cut into the middle of one of Cortinas' sentences.

"Who owns the building next door?"

"It's owned by a Chinese family in San Francisco. He used to run a restaurant. He died about three months ago. His family want me to rent it for them."

"It's about the only building on Bullard that's vacant, isn't it?"

"Yes, it is."

"How come you haven't rented it?"

"Even the so-called educated Mexican is, at heart, a superstitious person, *Senor* Regan. This Chinaman had a Mexican mistress."

"*Si?*"

"She suddenly died about four months ago. She and the Chinaman had had some loud and big arguments. Some claim Sam poisoned her. The Mexicans wouldn't eat at Sam's, afraid of more poison."

Regan smiled thinly.

"Then about a month ago Sam dies suddenly. That made it worse. Rumor said he'd poisoned himself. I don't know. I don't care."

"I've got to have an office here in town," Regan said.

"Want to look at it?"

"Sure."

The building was about a hundred feet long and forty feet wide. It smelled of greasy food, cobwebs and dust. There was a long plank counter and behind it shelves that had apparently held dishes and other cafe equipment.

"How much?" Regan asked.

"They want seventy-five ore a month. I'll rent it for sixty and keep ten for myself. I'm a ruthless bastard when it comes to business."

"I've guessed that."

Back in Cortinas' office the editor said, "I'm a nosey man. All newspaper men have long noses. But you have no freight to haul. You apparently can't get any, either. Why then this office?"

"Got to have one," Regan said.

Cortinas took the money, gave him a receipt and the key. "You're in business," he said. "Now, a few more questions."

After the interview, Regan went to the New Mexico House. The clerk came out of a side room. "Where's Margo?" Regan asked.

"Go up the stairs, turn right. Her room is next to the bathroom you used the first day in town. But she'll be making beds

215

now. A bed will be close and she'll be willing."

Regan slapped him across his ugly face. The man went back against the wall, anger flaring in his yellow eyes.

"Mister, you walk almighty high!"

"Keep a civil tongue," Regan snarled.

Regan climbed the creaking stairs, turned down the musty hall. Margo was bent over a bed making it. Regan watched her for some moments before she became aware of his presence.

"You look for Margo?"

"Yes."

"You come back for—"

Regan shook his head, smiling slightly. "How much a day does this stinking hotel pay you?"

"Dos pesos."

"One lousy Americano dollar. Can you keep your children and live on that?"

She shook her head. "That is why I wanted money from you for the use of me. I am not bad at heart."

Regan thought, They all say that, and he said, "Two bucks a day for working

216

for me. I take it you know almost every Mexican in town, don't you?"

"I was born here. I know them all."

"Two dollars," Regan repeated. He took four silver dollars from his pocket. "Two days in advance. Tell the clerk at the desk and come with me."

Her brown eyes studied him. "I have a steady job here. I do not want to work for only a few days and then have no job. They would not let me come back to this hotel."

"You'll have a steady job. You know where the empty building is next to the newspaper. Meet me there."

"*Si, Senor.*"

When she came into the building ten minutes later, Regan awaited her with a scrub bucket, a mop, and a broom. "Clean the joint out," he said. He handed her two more dollars. "You'll need some soap. I forgot to buy some. Whatever you need get at Valenzuela's store."

"You start the cafe?"

"Maybe. Maybe not."

He went outside. Old Wad came from

a cantina. "Had a beer," he explained, as though explanation were necessary. "What's going on in there?"

"Got Margo cleaning up. Our office."

"Hell, we ain't got no freight to haul. What good is an office?"

"We *might* get some freight," Regan said.

They got their horses and rode out of Silver City. When they rode past the office of New Mexico Wagons Regan glimpsed the red hair of Maria de Cordova behind her desk, for the big front window was shiningly clean. She raised her head and looked at him. Then Regan rode out of sight from her, a queer catch in his breast.

It was hell they had to be on different sides. He looked at the sun. It was low over the western horizon, shooting brilliant light across the mountainous desert.

He thought of the ultimatum Juan de Cordova had issued through Judge Alberto Gonzales. He remembered the toad-like ugly judge, squatting behind his desk. Juan de Cordova would not return until tomorrow. The judge would make no disastrous move without de Cordova in town. Sheriff Lucas Garcia would keep out of this, if possible. Gonzales would not order Garcia to ride out to the Williams *rancho* with a posse to drive his mules away, unless de Cordova was in Silver City to back the judge up.

The night should be peaceful. God knows he needed a night of good sleep.

He yawned.

11

THE heavily-laden wagon-train inched its way across the desert toward the Pinos Altos Mountains, dim blue peaks still some thirty miles to the northwest, and Regan, riding point on his mules, saw the dust of it before he made out the wagons—the yellow desert dust hanging against the brassy bowl of the torrid sky.

He let the mules drift by him and Morrison, Old Wad and Pedro gathered around him, horses sweaty and blowing.

"Wagons up ahead coming this way, men. That'll be New Mexico Wagons coming home from El Paso."

Old Wad sent him a hurried glance. "Juan de Cordova will probably be riding shotgun for them."

"He might be," Regan said. "Swing the mules to the west to let the wagons go by."

220

He loped along the line of mules, turning them west onto the desert, off the rutted wagon road. His face was dusty and grim. True to Old Wad's prediction, Juan de Cordova rode a sorrel gelding leading his wagons, a Winchester across the fork of his Chihuahua saddle in front of him.

Regan rode over to him.

Juan de Cordova pulled in his horse and his dark eyes raked Regan. He wore a light blue silk shirt, and he was clean-shaven. His eyes showed tiredness.

Regan pulled his horse close to de Cordova's.

"I got your ultimatum to get off Williams' land, de Cordova. I tore the order up and threw it in your fat judge's face."

Juan de Cordova's jaw tightened. His dark eyes were steady against Regan's.

"Make a move toward harming that *rancho* or my mules," Regan said clearly, "and I'm holding you liable for all damages—and you alone."

Juan de Cordova said nothing.

"Do I make myself clear?" Regan demanded.

"You do," Juan de Cordova said. "But did it ever occur to you, Senor Regan, that that order came from the Court, and if the Court is thrown to one side, there is no Law in this Territory?"

"You've made your own law . . . so far. I don't like your judge, your sheriff, or your law, de Cordova. So from here on out I'm making my own laws until this thing gets settled one way or the other—and then there'll be a law that favors all men, regardless of religion or color or birthplace."

"You might not live that long."

Regan said, "I'm here. In front of you. And I'm alive."

Juan de Cordova stiffened slightly, eyes suddenly glowing. Regan became tense, muscles controlled, eyes missing nothing. For a moment he thought de Cordova would swing up the Winchester. Just then a man loped in beside de Cordova. He was a heavy-set, bearded man and Regan had seen him around New Mexico Wagons office.

"Need some help, boss?"

Juan de Cordova shook his head. "Get back to your work, Charlie." His voice was sharp.

Charlie hesitated momentarily, eyes on Jim Regan, and then he turned his horse, riding toward the approaching wagons. From the corner of an eye, Regan noticed Old Wad and Morrison. They had pulled in their horses about a hundred feet away and were watching.

Regan said, "We're trailing mules into El Paso to pick up wagons. We're not leaving the country, de Cordova."

"What good are wagons if you have no freight to haul?"

"I'll figure that out. You just keep yourself and your hired crooks off Williams' property."

"I heard you the first time."

Regan swung his horse and rode away toward the mules. Morrison took the point and Regan put his horse beside Old

Wad's. Old Wad said, "That de Cordova fellow—that Charlie."

Regan glanced at him. "What about Charlie?"

"Right after you and Morrison headed out for Mogollon, this Charlie fellow went up to the ruins of the Santa Margarita Rancho. He hung around there a couple of days."

"Who told you this?"

"Reynolds. He saw him there. Reynolds' dog, that Constantinople mutt, barked one night, and Reynolds sneaked out, and this Charlie fellow was heading north alone on horseback."

Regan scowled.

"Well, Reynolds trailed him. This Charlie bucko made camp back in the boulders back of the Santa Margarita ruins. Reynolds said Charlie was still there when the 'paches chased Reynolds out. But he must've been wrong—them 'paches must've chased out Charlie, too."

Regan nodded. He rubbed his jaw. "What did Reynolds make of it? Maybe this Charlie went out on a mining expedition?"

"Not according to Reynolds. Charlie didn't have no pick or shovel or burro with him. Just some grub and his rifle."

Regan's jaw toughened. "So he went out there to lay an ambush for me and Morrison, huh? Get us when we came back on the wagon road. But the Apaches ran him off and besides, we came back across country."

"That's what Reynolds figured," Old Wad said. He loped to one side to turn an errant mule back into the bunch. He swung in again. "But who could prove that? Reynolds could be wrong."

"He'd have no other reason for hiding in those ruins," Regan said shortly. "Juan de Cordova's slipped him a few bucks."

"De Cordova backed down today. But maybe the next time he won't."

"Suits me," Regan grunted.

He gave himself over to watching the New Mexico Wagons train go past. Heavy Studebaker freighters were hooked together by chains in pairs. The tongue of the second wagon was chained to the reach of the wagon ahead. The lead wagon had six spans of mules hitched tandem. The wagons were heavily laden. Dirty canvas tarps covered their loads. Wheels ground desert dust, mules were shiny with sweat.

Regan counted six sets of wagons chained together. Twelve wagons, then, all heavily loaded . . . lots of freight. By tying two wagons together, de Cordova got by with only six skinners, not twelve. He'd heard in Silver City that de Cordova had doubled the pay of his men to get them to freight through this Apache backyard. To compensate for the double-wages he had tied wagons together, making one skinner do the work ordinarily done by two. He wondered, idly, how the crew liked this.

But those were Juan de Cordova's problems, not his. He had enough problems of his own, he thought sourly.

They pushed the mules as fast as possible. The week on pasture had added weight to them and renewed their endurance. When the afternoon sun got too hot they siestaed and drove all night, taking siesta the next forenoon when the sun again gained terrible heat. They covered the one-hundred and fifty miles to El Paso in three days, getting there in the evening of the third day.

Morrison led them to a Mexican who farmed on the north bank of the Rio Grande. The Mexican had run a ditch out of the Big River and had a hundred acres in alfalfa and head crops. He would graze their livestock for ten cents a head per day. They could also sleep in his bunkhouse, and this for free. His woman would feed them for twenty cents a meal.

After supper, Morrison rode toward El Paso, about a half mile away, and Regan and Old Wad sat on the bench, talking to the Mexican. He spoke broken English, so Regan encouraged him to speak in Spanish.

"When I came here, four years ago, this land was desert with chamisal and sagebrush, but I levelled it and took in water—and look at it now." The Mexican sucked his old pipe thoughtfully. "All any of this land needs is only water. Because of the sun it will grow anything, if it has water."

Regan remembered the wilderness in the canyon of the San Francisco River below Mogollon. Water—and work—could transform that land into a farm just this good.

The Mexican told them how to find Ramosa's *casa*. Regan and Old Wad rode into El Paso at dusk. Mexican children, some naked, played in the plaza, their childish voices shrill, and senoritas walked with their senores, the married couples with their children around them. They found Senor Ramosa's house, an adobe that bore well the marks of time, and the fat senor admitted them into his parlor, smiling and expressing surprise that Senor Regan had come after his wagons.

"I thought the Apaches had changed your mind," he said.

Ramosa talked of the three wagons the Apaches had burned, how dear to him the skinners of those wagons had been, how he prized each mule that had been slaughtered, and a few times he crossed his ample bosom profusely. Regan waited, knowing the slowness with which an Americano dealt with a Mexican, and, at the proper time, he brought out the subject of the other wagons—the ones Ramosa had made that were in his shop.

Ramosa had ten wagons made. Would the Senor Regan take them all? Would the Senor Regan take any? If Senor Regan did not want them, he had a ready market for them to a freighter who freighted between El Paso and Chihuahua, and that freighter wanted to buy them—but he was waiting for Senor Regan's decision.

Regan knew the Mexican *comerciante*. He doubted if Ramosa had any other possible sale for the wagons. How much did Senor Ramosa want per wagon? Senor Ramosa got paper and pencil. He went to his desk and made figures. Regan glanced at Old Wad. Old Wad winked at him.

Ten minutes went by. Back in the kitchen the cook rattled pans. The gigantic adobe house was quiet. Ramosa looked up suddenly, then named his price. Regan knew he had deliberately priced each wagon a hundred dollars too high. He deliberately offered two hundred dollars less than Ramosa wanted. The dickering began, continued, went on for an hour, and they split the difference, which was the original price Regan had intended to pay, and probably the original price Ramosa had put on each wagon.

Regan bought eight wagons. "I'll need harnesses, too," he said.

"Come back tomorrow. To my shop. I think I know where I can get you good harness—Nueva Leon leather—and cheap."

Outside, Old Wad sighed. "Too bad we ain't got nothing to haul back in those wagons."

Regan said nothing.

Old Wad wet his lips, looking at a cantina. A roar of voices and music came out of it. "Wonder where Morrison is?"

"Why not go out and look for him?"

That was just what the old man wanted. "See you later," he said.

Regan rode back to the farm. Night was thick with shimmering stars and the Rio Grande gurgled and had the smell of tules and cat-tails. The Mexican sat beside the bunk-house on the bench, smoking in the dark. Regan sat beside him.

"The nicest part of God's day," the Mexican murmured.

From within the house Regan could hear the voice of the Mexican's *senora* putting the children to bed. A strong unrest arose within him, coloring his thoughts with vivid hues. It was the hunger of a man for a home, for a wife, for a family. To belong to other humans, to have his feet on his own soil, to take his living from that soil.

He thought of Eleanor. He had wanted this with Eleanor. But she had been nothing but a gaudy moth, lured to the flame by momentary desire, nothing substantial. Those five months married to her had not been happy. Always there had been a conflict of desires, of will. She had divorced him, and he was glad of that.

Two people who should never have married had married. A mistake, from beginning to end, but a bitter mistake. Because of Eleanor, he thought of Maria de Cordova. He saw the red hair—the *rubia*—the curve of her glorious throat, the crisscross of lights in her dark eyes. He remembered the first time he'd met her on New Mexico Wagons' sidewalk, the day he'd come into Silver City, for the first time, and had roughed up Juan de Cordova.

But he had to get his thoughts from her.

"You will rest tomorrow, *senor?*" The Mexican had a soft voice. "You have about you the look of a tired man—a man who drives himself, and whose life is not happy." He puffed on his pipe for a long moment. "I should not have said that. It is none of my business."

"But I thank you, *senor.*"

"Your bed is waiting. Tomorrow we shall talk again."

Regan went to his bunk. He had trouble getting to sleep. About three, Old Wad came in, smelling of *tequilla*. The old man hit the bed and went to sleep instantly. Morning came. Morrison had not turned in.

"Prob'ly learning Spanish from some *senora*," Old Wad said. "I got a head on me that needs a barrel to hold it together. I'm not as young as I used to be."

"Thank God for that," Regan joked.

After breakfast they rode to Ramosa's wagon shop. Regan inspected the wagons carefully with Ramosa watching him and talking. The wheels were sturdy enough, the axles heavy for great weights, but Regan did not like the reaches—they were not made of heavy enough oak, he said. He and Ramosa talked back and forth. Regan would not take the wagons unless they had new and heavier reaches made for them.

Ramosa shrugged, "It will take two days."

"I'll wait."

"It will take twenty dollars more per wagon."

Regan shook his head. "We made a price. I hold you to it."

Ramosa considered, then agreed. Regan and Old Wad went out into the warm sunshine. Old Wad said, "Shall I look for Morrison?"

"You need a drink," Regan said. "You shake like a leaf in a windstorm."

Old Wad went into a *cantina*. Regan had the address of a harness maker, the one recommended by Ramosa, but he did not go into that harness shop. He did not trust Ramosa's judgment, for he knew it was tempered by getting a money kickback from the harness maker for sending him.

He dickered in that shop, went to another, then to the one Ramosa had recommended, made a survey, got bids on sixty harnesses, telling the makers to think it over, he would see them tomorrow.

He then went into a big mercantile store, the largest in town. He asked for

234

the owner, who turned out to be a tall, funereal looking Mexican, plainly from a long descent of Spanish dons.

Regan talked to the man, introduced himself, presented his proposition, and they spent the forenoon in the merchant's office. They had lunch together, the man's mozo bringing in food, and the afternoon was spent the same, and it was five when Regan came out of the establishment, his checking account badly shrunken.

Old Wad found him. "Where you been? Been looking for you."

"Where's Morrison?"

"He's been looking for you, too. All the saloons and everywhere. Morrison's not so dumb. He's got four men for you. Tough lookers, too, for skinners and a crew."

Morrison was in a *cantina*. Regan looked the men over. Morrison said, "I freighted with three of them—Carlos, Matthew, Johnson—out of Chihuahua. That fourth one, that Enrico fellow, I don't know. The others are tough. But they want double wages. Apaches."

Regan nodded.

Next morning, Regan bought the harnesses. Heavy tugs, thick belly bands, good collar pads, strong collars. The dealer hauled them to the farm in two wagons. Mules were driven in, harnessed, strung out. Soon they were hooked to the Ramosa wagons, four spans to a wagon, two wagons lashed together. Old Wad scratched his bald head.

"If we only had something to haul back in them." He laughed angrily. "Empty wagons."

"Get up," Regan ordered. "Follow me."

He went up on the high seat and jerklined his mules into action. Then with the other wagons following, he went down an alley lined with the backs of adobe buildings and peons who watched from paneless windows, with children running to get out of the way of the mules and wagons, until he came to the merchant's warehouse's loading-platform, where the merchant waited. There he whoaed his mules to a halt.

"What's going on?" Old Wad asked from his perch on the second wagon.

"Get down, and get to work."

He got the four new hands off to one side, while Morrison and Old Wad helped the merchant's crew fill the wagons. He dickered with them and settled the question of the amount of wages they would draw down, then they also started loading.

"Who you haulin' all this junk for?" Old Wad asked. "I didn't know you had an order out of Silver City. Which one of the bastards broke down and became human?"

"Here's the manifest bill," Regan told him. "Check it with Senor Alvarez there as they load."

"You ain't answered my questions."

Regan said, "See you in a few minutes."

He went between two buildings and came out on the main street. He entered the Federal Building and found the US

Land Agent. They went to the big wall map and Regan found the land below Mogollon. His finger travelled up the San Francisco River, stopped.

"Right about there."

No government survey had been run in this area, the clerk said, but it was open for homesteading. "The survey will be run later, I suppose, after this damn' Apache trouble quiets down and a survey group can get in there. We can straighten out your homestead lines then, I suppose."

When he left the office, an hour later, he owned a handful of legal papers and the chance to own six hundred and forty acres of land—a section—if he followed the homestead entry requirements.

By one o'clock the eight wagons were loaded, the bill paid, and the wagons rolled out of El Paso, heading northwest. Regan had put the four new men on the skinners' seats, their saddle-horses tied behind the wagons, and he and Old Wad and Morrison rode scout, with Regan riding ahead of the wagons and Old Wad on the left, Morrison on the right.

The morning of the fourth day out they met New Mexico Wagons headed toward El Paso—seven wagons rolling across the desert, five heavily laden with broken mill machinery going back east for repair work. Wagon freight etiquette demanded that the down-hill wagons would go into siding, letting the up-hill freight plod by.

But New Mexico Wagons made no move to pull its wagons to one side. Regan saw this and spurred in, right hand raised. Behind Juan de Cordova the freight wagons came to a halt.

"I'm taking the up-hill grade," Regan reminded quietly.

Juan de Cordova was one day out of Silver City. He was clean shaven, face blue from a close razor, and no dust covered his black pants or polished boots.

"You forget one thing," he reminded, "I'm loaded. You're empty."

Regan smiled tightly. "You're mistaken there, de Cordova. I'm loaded, and I'm climbing grade—and damn you, move your wagons, hear me?"

Juan de Cordova hesitated. His white teeth touched his bottom lip. His eyes were masked fire. He saw Regan's wagons well now, saw the tarps tied over the loads, and Regan thought he saw the man's eyes change from anger to curiosity.

Juan de Cordova had four scouts out, two on each side of his wagons. Regan saw them begin to move in. Morrison and Old Wad were moving in with them, and it looked for a moment that this would be fought out here on the desert.

Behind Juan de Cordova a mule stamped fighting blowflies. The sound was loud in the desert stillness.

Then Juan de Cordova said softly. "Never knew you were loaded, *Senor* Regan," and he stood on his stirrups, waving his skinners to take the west side.

Then he rode on, straight in his saddle, rifle across the saddle's fork, for all the world unaware of Regan and Regan's eight wagons with their sweaty toiling forty-eight mules.

Regan let his breath out slowly.

At two that afternoon, Regan's wagons came into Silver City. People stood under wooden awnings and watched. They moved past the office of New Mexico Wagons, and through the clean big window, Regan could see Maria de Cordova standing watching. He lifted his hand slightly, and he thought she nodded in return, but he could not be sure.

He pulled the lead wagon to a halt in front of the building he had rented. Margo came out, followed by three of her boys. She said, "The place is clean.. There were many *cucarachas*. The cockroaches. But they are gone now."

Regan swung out of saddle. To Morrison he said, "Get the boys busy unloading." He gestured toward the building. "Everything goes inside. You need more help?"

Sheriff Lucas Garcia stood watching from the doorway of Cortinas' newspaper office, Cortinas standing beside him.

Banker Lamas watched from the window of his bank. Across the street Matthew Valenzuela stood in the doorway of his Mercado, watching.

Maria de Cordova crossed the street to stand beside Regan. She did not come to his shoulders, Regan noticed. He looked down at her glistening red hair.

She lifted her dark eyes. "I know we're supposed to be enemies," she said quietly, "but let's lay that aside for a moment, *Senor* Regan. What in the name of heaven are you doing? Those men carrying everything into this building—"

"I'm starting a store."

Old Wad stood within earshot. He turned with wide eyes. "So that's what you're doing, eh? Well, don't look at me —I won't clerk in it, I can tell you that!"

Maria de Cordova laughed.

Regan smiled. "Did I ask you to?" he asked.

12

A BEARDED man had come out of New Mexico Wagons' office. Regan spoke to Maria de Cordova.

"That fellow named Charlie Parks?"

She looked at the bearded man. Her eyes came back to him. "Yes, that's his name." Something in his stern face scared her. "Why did you ask?"

"This Parks was gone a few days, wasn't he? When Morrison and I made the Mogollon run?"

She hesitated, wondering. "Yes."

Regan crossed the street toward Charlie Parks. The entire thing, in his mind, had become simple—he had to hit at New Mexico Wagons first, beat Juan de Cordova to the punch. He had to put aside his feelings toward Maria.

"Your name Charlie Parks?"

"Yes?"

"You were hiding out in the Santa Margarita ruins a few days last week, Parks. You were seen out there. You had a rifle, but no pack mule, just a saddle-horse. You weren't prospecting, because you never had a pick and shovel."

Parks' eyes showed metallic glints. "What are you drivin' at, Regan?"

Jim Regan spoke slowly. "You were out there hiding to ambush me and Morrison on our return trip to Silver City. But we fooled you through luck—we sold our mules there, left our wagons in Mogollon, and cut across country—so you missed us."

Charlie Parks said, "You're loco."

"Juan de Cordova hired you to put up an ambush, Parks. I've got a bit of advice for you."

"Yeah . . . an' that?"

"Watch your step from here on out."

Parks' bearded mouth opened in a silent laugh. "You walk almighty big, Regan. But maybe you ain't as big as you think you are!"

Parks had his hand on his holstered gun.

Regan hit him in the mouth—a hard jolting blow. Gun rising, Parks went back, and Regan stepped in, wrestling the pistol from Parks' grip. The door of the office of New Mexico Wagons was open. Regan tossed the pistol through the door. It hit the floor with a clatter.

Parks spat blood. "You got the jump on me," he accused.

"Next time I won't let you off so easy," Regan said.

Sheriff Lucas Garcia jammed his soft bulk between them. "What's goin' on here?"

"None of your damn' business," Regan said.

Garcia's eyes became stormy. "You're not the law here, Regan."

Regan smiled. "You stupid jackass, wake up and die right! There is no law here, but what a man makes for himself. I never tore the badge off you that day just for exercise."

"We'll see about that," Garcia threatened.

"Call all the town council meetings you want," Regan invited. "None of them will make a bit of difference with me." He lifted his eyes to Parks, who was daubing blood from his beard with a dirty red bandanna. "Just keep in mind what I told you, Parks."

Parks had no reply. His eyes were red and sullen.

Quite a crowd had hurriedly gathered. Regan moved through the people, eyes on Maria de Cordova. He tried to guess at what ran behind her brown eyes. He guessed a grudging admiration rode there, and also there was something livid and bright, and he read this as fear.

Her lips opened. Regan thought she was going to say something. But she turned and walked toward New Mexico Wagons' office, without a word.

Morrison said, "You jumped at conclusions," and his voice was low.

"What else could a man think?"

Morrison tugged his beard. "Juan de Cordova's his boss," he reminded gently.

Regan only nodded.

Matthew Valenzuela walked over from his store. "They tell me I'm going to have competition." His voice was thin.

"No freight to haul . . . for me," Regan said. "So, I go into business." He let the words hang—an open challenge.

"I've noticed Margo and her biggest kids parading through my store. Wondered what they wanted. Now I can see they were looking at my prices. I suppose you'll keep your prices in line with mine?"

Regan shook his head. "You have a hundred per cent markup, Valenzuela. You sell at double your cost. I'm selling at one-half again the cost. No more."

Anger made the merchant's cheekbones stand out. "You'll go broke," he threatened. "You can't haul merchandise all the way from El Paso and run on such a small margin."

"I'll be the one who goes broke."

"Who's going to run your store?"

247

Regan had spent long hours debating on this point himself. On the trip into El Paso and back, this problem had ridden on the high seat with him.

"Margo."

"She's just a dumb ignorant Mexican chambermaid. She knows nothing about merchandising—keeping books and that."

The old Silver City hierarchy. The *comerciante* versus the *peon*. "I'll keep the books," Regan assured.

"These Mexicans will steal you blind. These Mexicans are all thieves."

"You should know. You're a Mexican."

Valenzuela's mouth made odd motions. Then he said, "Looks to me like you don't want a friend in this town."

"I'll soon have lots of friends. All the so-called peons will buy at my store. They don't make much money—scab wages paid by your mines. Every cent counts to them, double. They'll buy from me, not you."

"When you go broke—and if you have

any stock left—come over and I'll take it off your hands."

"Thanks. I'll do that."

Valenzuela turned without another word and went to his store. Regan glanced at him, smiling whimsically, and then he became aware of Joseph Cortinas standing beside him, watching the men unload the wagons.

"Think you'll break this local royalty in two, *Senor* Regan?"

"I'm going to try."

"I'm a business man," Cortinas said, "always out for the thing with Uncle Sam's signature on it—that green stuff. How about selling you a nice fat ad?"

"I'll see you in a little while."

"I'll be there," Cortinas smiled. "With my safe open to receive your cash."

Cortinas left and a stocky middle-aged man moved over and said, "I'm General Humberto Gonzales. I'm in charge of the local militia."

Regan looked down into a wide dark face broken by red blood vessels. The idea came that *Senor* Gonzales loved his bottle.

"I've heard of you. You've sort of pushed Lucas Garcia off the white throne, they tell me."

General Gonzales spoke stiffly. "I merely handle the militia. To defend the town against Apaches is my job."

"Apaches won't hit this town. For one thing there are too many people here to buck up against. Another thing is—what would they want in this town?"

"Grub. Bullets. Rifles."

Regan shook his head. "They can get all three of them off the stages and wagon trains. And stand less chance of losing lives, too. You people all act like these Apaches are animals—dumb, ignorant, stupid. They're people, and they're not dumb."

"But they haven't hit any wagons yet. Only the stage."

"That's because they're over west in the Chiricahua Mountains. They're banding up in one big bunch. That's common talk in El Paso."

Gonzales cracked a knuckle. "This town will only take so much, *Senor* Regan. I say that not only from the standpoint of a law enforcement officer, I base that upon long experience in handling men in the armed forces."

"You aren't in the army now. You're a civilian."

Gonzales sent him a hard look, then turned and walked away. Regan went into the store to supervise the unloading of the merchandise. Margo and her children had cleaned the old building until it glistened. Newspapers had been laid upon shelves. Most of the material was in wooden crates.

"Take that easy," she scolded Morrison. "That might have dishes in it."

Morrison shoved back his hat. His lips wore a battered grin. "You look almighty nice to my eyes, Margo. You got a husband, ain't you?"

"None of your business."

Regan gestured and Margo followed him to the back room. The Chinaman had used this for an office. Regan sank down in the swivel chair and motioned for her to sit in the other chair.

"You know about everybody in town, you tell me. You're going to be boss here —under me."

She nodded, eyes wide.

"I got manifest bills for everything we hauled up from El Paso. Once a week I'll take inventory. If I find so much as a cookie missing I'm going to send you walking."

"There will be no stealing. For a long time I have wanted a job like this. But because I was a Mexican peon I had to scrub floors and make beds—"

Regan cut her short. "And none of that stuff you tried to pull on me that day you washed my back."

She blushed suddenly, looking at her work-worn hands. "I did it for two reasons. I liked you. I needed the money so bad."

"No more of that?" Regan thought, Hell, I sound like a father lecturing a child.

She raised her dark eyes. "No more of that . . . unless with you."

Oh, God, Regan thought.

"But I should not have said that. You are for the grand lady, the Senorita Maria de Cordova. All the town talks about how she looks at you."

Regan stared. Finally he clipped shut his mouth. "That's all," he said. "We open for business at eight in the morning. I'll work with you tonight marking tags and prices."

"We will make much money for you. Every peon in Silver City will buy if your prices are lower than Senor Valenzuela's. I know every Mexican family—the poor ones—in Silver City."

"Good. Now get to work."

He leaned back and watched her leave the room. He wondered if she were not losing weight. Her hips were broad but her waist seemed narrower. His throat felt light and uncomfortable. He knew he could have her any time he wanted her. But once he had her—

He shook his head. She'd then follow

the pattern of all women—she would own him, think she could boss him.

None of that, he decided, although it would be fun. He was checking the manifest bills when he heard Margo say "A gentleman to see you, *Senor* Regan."

Regan had never seen the man before. He was a powerful-looking man, with huge shoulders and thick torso. He had a wide, homely face, and his nose, once broken, had not healed properly, turning off to the right.

Regan invited him to sit down. The man shook his head. "My name is Mike O'Henry. I tend bar at Madame Beauvrais place. You know Madame Beauvrais, don't you?"

Regan shook his head. "Never had the pleasure, O'Henry, but I've heard of her place. I've heard Juan de Cordova owns an interest in it."

O'Henry shook that aside. "Maybe he does, and maybe he doesn't. I never came here to talk about *Senor* de Cordova. The madame sent me to ask you if you'd be kind enough to drop in this afternoon and see her?"

Regan shook his head. "You know, this is an odd thing, *Senor* O'Henry, but I've never been in a house of ill-fame in my life—just never got around to it, I guess —and I kind of figure I'm too old now to get such a bad habit, if only to see the madame of the joint."

"You won't come?"

"No."

O'Henry rubbed his broken nose. He showed a tight little smile. "That's positive?"

"You're a hard man to convince." Regan studied him. "Now why would the madame want to see me?"

"I don't know. She just told me to go and see you."

Regan nodded. "Thanks."

O'Henry left. Regan went out and talked to Old Wad. "Ride out to the ranch and see how things are. We've got enough hands here unloading."

"We got one wagon already unloaded. I'll drive it out."

"Okay."

Regan was sitting in his office, when the woman came in the back door. She was small, thin waisted, with pitch-black hair, but her mouth was a little too hard, the lines around it rapidly forming. Regan got to his feet, gestured toward a chair, and said, "You're Madame Beauvrais?"

"Yes." She sat down, dark eyes on him. He liked the way her tiny hat, with its long ostrich plume, sat on her dark hair. "You are not very polite, Mister Regan."

"Blame it on my Irish parents."

She looked at her tiny hands. "I'll go straight to the point. You seem to be a man of few words. I came here to talk about Juan de Cordova."

Regan had half-expected this. He waited.

"Day by day, things get worse between you and Juan. Juan is fighting for something his family has held for years. Juan is a stubborn man, Senor Regan."

"I'm sort of stubborn too, they tell me."

"I'm afraid Juan—or you—or maybe both of you—might get killed. I'll go a step further. I love Juan de Cordova."

Her strained face showed she meant every word.

Regan was at a loss for words. The strangeness of this hit him—a prostitute in love with a member of an old Spanish family, a proud family, the royal family of Silver City.

"Did Juan de Cordova send you to see me?"

Anger touched her face, making tiny cheekbones stand out. "That was a cruel thing to say."

"De Cordova is a cruel man, Miss Beauvrais. He is a ruthless man, a cold man. He is, as you say, also stubborn. But I still cannot see why you came to me? What can I do?"

"You can leave, *Senor* Regan."

Regan shook his head. "That's out of the question. To me the statement is pure folly. There is freight here to be hauled by both of us. Juan de Cordova will give me none of that freight. I'm starting a store. I hope to make money on it. I won't leave."

She hesitated. "How much would it be worth to you—to leave?"

Regan at last saw through her game. "You can't buy me, Miss Beauvrais. You said that Juan de Cordova is a stubborn man. Well, I'm just as stubborn. You can't buy me. You can't scare me." His smile softened. "So I guess I'm a right hard man to deal with, am I not?"

She got to her feet. "I've gained nothing."

"Oh, yes, you have. You've gained and I've gained. We both see how the other stands. And I have had the opportunity to meet a fine person, Miss Beauvrais."

"Do you mean that?"

"I certainly do."

Her red lips twisted. "The Irish in you, Senor Regan. But I thank you just the same."

"The pleasure was mine."

She looked at the wall beyond him. "I should leave this town. I should pack up and sneak off like the whore I am. I build dreams. He wouldn't marry me."

"He'll be foolish if he doesn't."

She smiled, then. "That was nice of you. I see there is no use talking any more. From now on its in the lap of God. And I don't think God cares too much. But I want one favor of you, *Senor* Regan."

"And that?"

"Nobody saw me come. Nobody but us two know what we talked about. Do not mention this to Juan. Or to Maria, either."

Regan grinned. "Juan won't hardly speak to me. Maria is worlds away."

"Maybe not as far as you think."

She left. Regan sat listening to her high heels move down the alley. He wiped his forehead. This was a loco world. Sometimes it bucked a man off right handily.

But there was no use sitting here thinking about it. There were certain facts each man had to accept. He went out into the store proper, saw things were going well, and went to Joseph Cortinas' office.

He composed an ad, copying down prices from a list Margo had made for him. Cortinas watched, smoking one of his endless cigarettes.

"You're one of my best customers," the printer finally said.

Regan said, "Then why not throw some hauling my way?"

Cortinas had a wooden dead face. He said nothing. Regan finished the ad. Cortinas would print it in the form of a handbill, and would get his newsboys to distribute it this evening. Regan paid him with check. He totalled his bank account. It had shrunken disastrously. The harnesses, the wagons, the loads of merchandise. He had been lucky to have been paid so well for the Mogollon trip. He realised he owed much to Enrique Williams.

He said to Cortinas, "You've heard about Juan de Cordova getting the judge to declare Enrique Williams a public nuisance, and the attempt to take Williams' *rancho* in as public property, I suppose?"

Cortinas nodded. "De Cordova is

reaching a little too far," he said slowly, and closed that discussion.

Regan said, "I'd hate to pull my wagons back to El Paso empty."

Cortinas sat down behind his desk, playing with a pencil. His eyes did not meet those of Regan. From the backshop came the sound of a printer hammering a form with a rawhide mallet.

Cortinas finally said, "I have nothing to haul to El Paso."

Regan stared at the blank wall. The power of Juan de Cordova was a living thing, harsh and strong. Regan felt anger, but held it. Stronger than anger in him, was the desire to whip de Cordova.

"Christ, I wish I had a hundred thousand bucks. I'd tip this complacent burg upside down. I'd run these merchants out of business, even if I had to give my things away."

Cortinas lifted troubled eyes. "You'd do it, too," he said quietly.

13

JUAN DE CORDOVA did not ride shotgun with his wagons all the way to El Paso. He left them at the first watering-spot, Tres Cabozas, and came back riding scout for the stage. Regan had gone back to Silver City with loaded wagons. What freight had those wagons contained? Had somebody in Silver City—one of the mines, a merchant, or even Joseph Cortinas—weakened? Was his hold on Silver City slipping?

He came in at dusk riding ahead of the stage. There had been no sign of Apaches. His nerves raw, he rode his sweaty horse into the compound, came down and hollered for the hostler, leaving his horse with trailing reins. He strode into New Mexico Wagons' office, a tall and powerful man, clothing dusty.

Maria was alone in the office.

"What did Regan haul back in those wagons?"

His voice was harsh. He saw anger touch her face, driving away her look of femininity.

"I'm not one of your peons."

He said bluntly. "I asked a question. I want an answer—a fast answer. What was in his wagons?"

"He's starting a store."

Juan de Cordova settled into a chair. He stuck out his dust-covered boots and looked at them. "He sure does want to stay in this town," he said thickly. "Where?"

"The building next to Cortinas' print shop."

"Cortinas rented it to him huh?" Juan de Cordova pulled in his boots, face showing hard planes. "That printer looked like he'd be the first one to break. I guess he and I should have a long talk."

"That'll do you no good."

He studied his sister under lidded eyes. "You seem to know so damn' much, maybe you should be running my business?"

"I couldn't do much worse."

"Who are you for? Me or Regan?"

"I'm not for you. You're tackling this wrong—completely wrong. There's plenty of freighting for both of you. You got more than you can handle."

"Then you're for Regan?"

"No."

"Then what the hell are you for?"

"For peace. I don't want you killed. I don't want *Senor* Regan killed. I don't want anybody killed. I'm for peace. Simple but necessary peace. That's where I stand."

"What's your great plan?" he scoffed.

"You and Regan combine. Work as a team. You got something bigger than each other here to fight. You got Apaches. You join teams, join men, run wagons together—"

"My sister," he said slowly. "My sister. The daughter of my father. Why the hell don't you go into a nunnery?"

"I might. I will, if for no reason than

264

to get this weight off my back. Juan, listen to reason."

"If you're talking *reason*, I've listened to too much of it."

"There's no use talking to you." She put on her rebozo, tugging the sarape across her small shoulders. "You know, I've never been in a whorehouse in my life, but I might walk into one right soon."

"You leave Beauvrais out of this!"

She had seen Madame Beauvrais go down the alley, and enter Regan's office. She almost mentioned this to her brother, but held her tongue. She did not want to cause Madame Beauvrais any trouble.

She shrugged. "As you say." She left.

Juan de Cordova sat for a few moments gazing at his boots and thinking. Then he went out into the compound. Charlie Parks left the commissary and came up to him.

"Regan jumped me," he said.

"What about?"

"Somehow he got wind of my being out there at Santa Margarita. He put two and two together, and he didn't get five. I went to pull my gun on him, but he beat me to it."

"With his gun?"

Parks rubbed his jaw. "Fist, Juan."

De Cordova said, "Why don't you kill him?"

"He's fast with a gun. He's hell with fists. He hit me so fast, I never saw it coming. Then his gun was on me—just like that."

Juan de Cordova said quietly, "This town has alleys. The night is getting darker."

"How much?"

There was a moment of silence. "Five hundred bucks," de Cordova said. "Dead."

"I'll think it over."

"He's got you marked," Juan de Cordova said. "Walk light. If you don't, he'll kill you."

"He might let it drop."

Juan de Cordova shrugged. "He might. Then again he might not. If you don't run against Regan, get t'hell out of Silver City."

"That an order?"

"An order," Juan de Cordova repeated.

He left Parks standing in the gathering dark. He went past Regan's new store to Cortinas' office. Cortinas was in the back, setting type and de Cordova went back to him.

"Busy, Joseph?"

"Setting an ad. Got to be out soon." De Cordova looked at his ink-black hands. "Regan's ad. His store."

"Think he'll dent Valenzuela's business?"

"Here's his sale list. At this rate he'll not dent it, he'll wreck it. Every miner's wife in the country will buy from him."

"You don't have to print it," Juan de Cordova said.

Cortinas looked at him with a slow smile. "Juan, I have to eat. I have to make money. You can take it for what it's worth—but you won't whip this gringo."

"He'll run out of money."

"Not as long as he runs this store—and

sells at these prices. Valenzuela might just as well close shop right now."

"You weakening, Joseph?"

"I'm a business man, nothing more. Where I can save money—I save money. Where I can make money—I make money. Regan has thrown a lot of money in advertising my way."

"Don't weaken."

Cortinas' fingers trembled as he put type into the case. He glanced at Juan de Cordova, seeing the tightness of the man's blocky jaw. He had a cold feeling in his belly. But this did not last long. From the alley behind the print shop came the sound of three shots.

Cortinas owned the newspaper man's impartial mind. Two shots were close together, he noticed, and the third and last was spaced a while after the second.

"What the hell—?" Cortinas said.

Juan de Cordova led the way out the back door. The alley was rather dark, but he saw a man lying in the gravel, toward his left. Regan leaned against the wall of his office, gun in hand.

Juan de Cordova heard people converging on the scene. Somebody came out of Regan's office carrying the lamp. Lamplight showed grizzled pain on Regan's face.

"What happened?" Cortinas asked.

"Somebody knocked on the door," Regan said. "I came outside. He'd gone up the alley a little ways. He shot at me. I shot at him. There he is up there."

"You get hit?" Cortinas asked.

"My leg," Regan said painfully. "My right leg, down low."

Juan de Cordova asked, "Who's the fellow that shot at you?"

"I don't know."

A group of men entered the alley. They saw the body lying there, and one man turned it over. "That's Charlie Parks," he said.

Juan de Cordova had a cold spot in his belly. Maybe Parks wasn't dead—maybe he could still talk—Parks had gone to work in a hurry. To hide his consternation Juan de Cordova walked to the dead man. He knelt beside him and saw that Parks was shot through the heart. He got to his feet, a thousand years of weight peeling off his shoulders.

"He's dead." He looked at Regan, who'd hobbled over, gun still in his hand. "You and he had words this afternoon, somebody told me."

Regan said, "He worked for you, de Cordova."

Juan de Cordova laughed quietly. "He was on my payroll, sure. But not as a gunman, Regan."

"I wonder. . . ."

Morrison had moved in beside his boss, one arm around Regan's waist. He cursed vividly and said, "We'd best get you to the doc, or get doc over here. Put your weight on me, Regan."

Regan said, "This may be the time."

Everybody knew what he meant. Juan de Cordova moved away slightly. But Morrison cut in with, "Boss, don't—not now. Here, damn you, come with me!" Bodily he turned Regan, and Morrison's face was pale in lamplight. "Margo, hold the lamp ahead of me."

Regan hobbled, blood in his boot. His leg was not broken, for it would hold his weight, although with sharp pain. He gritted his teeth, grinding them, fighting the pain, and he was still gritting his teeth, face pale, when the doctor came in.

"Not now," Morrison kept saying, "not now, Regan."

Morrison and the doctor cut off Regan's boot, slitting it down the outside seam. Regan leaned over and looked at the wound. The bullet had gone about one-half an inch into the calf of his leg, ripped out a chunk, and then gone on.

"Juan de Cordova hired him," Regan said.

Morrison shook his head. "You weren't in any condition to take him on out there. You'd've worked into his hands, boss."

Regan leaned back in his chair. He knew that Morrison was right. Besides, he had no proof de Cordova had put Parks' gun against him. He remembered hitting Parks, driving him back, wresting his gun from him, and he remembered the ugly hate that had flared across Parks' bearded face. Juan de Cordova might not have had to spur Parks.

Sheriff Lucas Garcia came in. "What happened?"

Morrison shoved him out the back door. "Talk to your boss, de Cordova," he said. He barred the door with the slidebolt. He wore a twisted whiskery grin.

Regan closed his eyes and fought stinging pain as the doctor put something on the wound, washing it. That sharp pain left and the leg felt better. When he opened his eyes he had tears in them.

"How long will I be laid up, doc?"

"A day or so, I guess. If I can keep infection off, and keep you still for a day."

Regan thought, God, I was lucky.

The doctor bound the wound. "He can't ride a horse for a day or so," he told Morrison.

"We'll take him home in the wagon."

"He shouldn't put his weight on his leg."

"I'll help," Margo said.

Between Margo and Morrison, they got Regan into a wagon that was already empty. Margo said, "I stay until the wagons are unloaded," and her wide face smiled. "You get well now, boss."

"Thanks," Regan said. "Lock up when you're unloaded."

"Tomorrow is a big day," Margo said.

Cortinas came out of his shop. "Your handbills will go out in the morning, Senor Regan. Too late tonight, but I'll get the boys first thing in the morning. How do you feel?"

"Doc says I'll live."

Cortinas searched Regan's face with sharp eyes. Regan got the impression he wanted to say more, but he did not. He went back into his shop.

Sheriff Garcia came from the alley. His wide fleshy face was livid with rage. "There'll be an inquest," he told Regan.

Regan looked down from the high seat. "Who'll conduct it?"

"Judge Alberto Gonzales, of course."

Regan smiled mirthlessly. He'd stand the chance of a snowball in hell in Judge

Gonzales' court. "You send the judge out to see me," he said. He spoke to Morrison. "Use the bullwhip."

Morrison cramped the teams and turned the wagon in the street, taking up the entire space. People scattered like scared hens in front of the leaders. They left Sheriff Garcia standing watching them.

Regan snorted, "Inquest, hell! There were only two of us in that alley—me and Parks."

"They might hire some witnesses," Morrison said.

"Juan de Cordova and Judge Gonzales aren't that stupid. They know better than to hold an inquest. There might be some of their own dirty wash hung on the line."

Morrison chuckled deeply.

The teams plodded. By driving slowly, Morrison did not disturb Regan's leg perched on the dashboard.

"You think Juan de Cordova hired Parks?"

"I don't know. If he did, nobody could prove it, least of all Parks. If I hadn't killed Parks, we might have found out something. But he's a dead man now."

They met Old Wad at the gate. The mules were all right, he said—he'd counted them as best he could in the dark. Reynolds and his brood were holding down the fort.

Old Wad opened the gate. "Thought you were going to move the wagons out in one bunch?"

"Others aren't unloaded," Regan said. "Have they seen any sign of Enrique Williams?"

Old Wad mounted his horse, after closing the gate. "Williams came in about an hour ago. Just come out of the brush. How come you hold your leg up against the dashboard thataway, Jim?"

Regan grinned. "Sprained my ankle."

14

REGAN told Williams about Judge Gonzales' court order. The man's face showed graven indecision. Finally he said, "I'd better not let the judge or Juan de Cordova get their hands on me."

Regan asked him about Mogollon. The town was still standing, an oasis in Apacheria. They were eating the mules. Regan thought of Sweet Jasmine. She would be tough chewing. Or maybe, he corrected himself, she *had been* tough chewing.

"They'll need more grub in about two weeks," Williams informed.

Regan said, "I think they'd better trek overland to Silver City. I doubt if we could freight more grub back to them. These Apaches are pretty bad. I heard in El Paso they'd sacked some big ranches over south of Tucson. The people of

Mogollon send you in to talk to us about more grub?"

Williams shook his long hair. "No. But two days ago I was hid in the brush between here and Mogollon, in a canyon. I seen these Apaches comin' and I hid in the brush before they saw me."

Everybody listened. Reynolds leaned on his long rifle, Constantinople sitting beside his master's boots. The children were grouped around the big room. The current Mrs. Reynolds listened from the kitchen door. Morrison and Old Wad squatted, backs to the wall. Regan sat with his bandaged leg resting on a chair.

"They watered their horses at the spring. They were talking about Cabazon."

Regan remembered Cabazon's grizzly head jammed on the nail down in Silver City. Desert heat had pulled the meat tightly to the high cheekbones. Some clown had wired back the corners of Cabazon's mouth to give the ghastly head an even more evil-looking appearance.

"They'd sent a runner over into

Arizona to tell Victorio about Cabazon's death, that you two killed him. And according to them, it wasn't a fair fight."

"What was wrong with it?" Morrison demanded hoarsely.

"You used dynamite, not rifles."

Sudden pain speared through Regan's leg. He grimaced. "They hardly fought fair, either," he pointed out. "They had us outnumbered right nicely, if I remember right."

"They don't take that into consideration. But don't forget that Victorio and Cabazon has tasted each other's blood. They've opened a vein on each other and lapped the other's blood. That makes them blood brothers. And that, to an Apache, is greater than being a born brother."

Morrison snorted loudly and openly.

"Don't laugh at it," Williams said.

Regan said, "Then you think Victorio and his gang might leave southeast Arizona and work over this way to get my scalp and Morrison's?"

"I'm just telling you what I heard."

They loaded Williams' burro with canned goods and grub, and he left at two in the morning. Regan was out on guard over the mules, and the man stopped and talked with him for a while. Williams was *close* to finding the Lost Adam mine. The next time he came in he'd know where the mine was, for sure. His voice rose a little when he mentioned the lost gold mine. Regan listened and said nothing. Each man to his own devices, he thought. Williams and his burro moved off into the warm New Mexico night. Two hours later, Morrison came out to relieve his boss.

"You set much stock by what Williams said about Victorio and Cabazon?" Morrison asked.

Regan smiled. "Hell, I'm no Apache, Morrison. I don't know how one thinks or feels. But I do know one thing—things have been too quiet on the trail. They've only hit that one stage. Juan de Cordova hauls through, and so far he's not lifted a rifle against an Apache."

Morrison rubbed his scar. His rough

fingers made bristling noises on his beard. The night was quiet. The mules grazed on the green alfalfa, dark spots in the dark night.

"And I know another thing," Regan said, "and that is we're going to have dynamite with us, a box under each wagon, both coming and going."

"Wonder if de Cordova is wise to that dynamite trick?"

"I doubt it. Only you and me—and the people in Mogollon—know how we got Cabazon and his bunch. I've told nobody. Nobody from Mogollon has been in Silver City to the best of my knowledge. And I don't think you told anybody."

"One of those Apaches must've got away."

"I think one did. I caught a glimpse of him, but couldn't get him. But hell, what difference does it make? Sooner or later those Apaches are going to hit one of our freight trains."

"Reckon it makes no never mind."

Regan reached for the willow he used as a cane. "I'm heading for my bunk."

He hobbled to his horse but did not mount him. To mount him would be difficult. His leg felt stiff. To swing it over a saddle might start the bleeding again. He limped into camp and went to bed. He was up at seven, and in town by eight.

Margo was just opening the new store. She wore a new dress, highly starched, and her hair was combed back severely, accentuating her wide dark face.

"The boys are delivering the hand-bills," she said. "I met two of them coming from home."

"Good."

Mill hands were climbing the mountain to the stamp mills. With only one shift a day running, a miner only worked every three days. Regan knew this had cut into their incomes rather severely. Of course each man made a few *pesos* by putting in his time in the militia, but this was not the same as working six and seven days a week.

They were mostly Mexicans, he noticed, with a few Irishmen and other nationalities. He found himself wondering why most of them did not leave with such few hours of work and subsequently small paychecks. Then he remembered the terror of the desert to the south. Union meant strength.

Two stood looking in the window at Margo's hastily-constructed window display. One of them, a Mexican, spoke in Spanish. "You sell cheap," he said. "Valenzuela has robbed us for years."

"Send your family in," Regan invited.

Margo had orders to give a sack of candy with each purchase, regardless of the size of that purchase. Play on the kids and you get the parents, Regan had told her, knowing that dulces was a sweet item not many of the local children could afford, because of the low wages of their fathers. Also most of these men had big families.

Margo and Regan went inside. "We are open for business," Margo said, stationing her bulk behind the counter.

Regan ran a sour eye over the interior. Things were a mess—this piled there, that piled over there. He had no taste for this merchandising business. He was a freighter, not a merchant. But then a stern determination surged through him, pulling at his arteries. He'd either make this town—these merchants, these mill owners—come to him, give him a living freighting out of this town, or he'd go broke and walk out, if need be. They'd asked for a fight. He'd given them one.

He hobbled back to his office and sat down. During the next hour Margo had only two customers. Regan had one visitor. She came down the alley. She stopped inside the door and leaned against it, face bright from walking, dark eyes glistening.

"How's your leg?"

Regan said, "Getting better, Miss Maria."

He found his heart beating rapidly. He looked at her cute chin, her red lips, her dark eyes. She smiled then, and the smile was soft, and he liked that, too. He cursed rough, tough, Fate. Why in the hell did she have to be Juan de Cordova's sister?

He got to his feet. She came only to his shoulders. He realised her tinyness, and he liked that, too. She looked up at him. Things happened rapidly, and to Regan's liking. Somehow, she was close to him, her perfume smelled nice, it fitted her smallness. And somehow then his arms got around her, and hers around him. Regan's fumbling lips found her fumbling lips. They were warm, they were moist, and they trembled, and he felt her arms tighten. Then they broke and looked at each other. Her eyes held small tears, he noticed.

"I knew this was coming," she said dreamily. "Ever since the day I first saw you, Jim. I'll admit it, I've been a ruthless wench." She laughed shakily. "I said to myself, 'There's the man I want. I only hope he wants me.' That's what I said, Jim. Isn't that terrible?" She nestled her head against his shoulder, burrowing in closer.

His throat was dry. "I guess I thought the same, Maria."

She glanced up at him quickly. "You *guess!*"

"You know, Maria, it seems as though I always say the wrong thing! I *knew*, not *guessed*."

"That's better."

Regan smiled. "You know, what I'm going to say isn't very romantic."

"What are you going to say?"

"My leg—It's hard to stand on it."

"Oh, I forgot all about it, Jim. Sit down, please." Her voice already held wifely concern. "Here, I'll help you, Jim."

He got in the Chinaman's old swivel chair. She pulled a chair close and sat with her knee almost touching his. Her dark eyes fed on his face. She had been lonely, he knew. Now that loneliness was at an end. He felt the same way—a warm, good feeling.

Suddenly her face clouded. She put her head in her hands and sobs shook her shoulders. Regan put a hand out and

285

found hers. There was nothing he could say or do. He knew why she wept. After a while she raised her head and daubed at her eyes with a small silk handkerchief.

"What if—you killed—my brother?"

Regan sat in silent and dumb misery.

"Jim, will you leave?"

Regan groaned in misery. Then he said, "There should be room for both of us. For your brother and me. I think we should go easy. Talk to him, Maria. Do you want me to go with you? To tell him about how we feel about each other?"

She considered that. Then she said, "No, I do not think the time is ripe. I ask one thing of you—do not provoke any more trouble. If he provokes trouble with you, then that is his fault."

Regan promised . . . and wondered if he could keep the promise. Now she seemed confused, utterly confused—the problem was so huge, so immense. She got to her feet.

"I shall have to go now. When I am near to you, I cannot think straight. I have been that way ever since meeting you, Jim."

Regan got to his feet. There was nothing he could say. She stopped at the door.

"Have I been a cheap woman, by throwing myself at you?"

He shook his head and smiled. "Sooner or later it had to happen. You did not throw yourself at me, Maria. We both threw ourselves at each other."

She kissed him hurriedly, eyes sparkling again, and left. The door had just closed behind her when Margo moved into the office. "The business is not good," she said.

"The handbills are hardly out yet," Regan reminded. "Women are cleaning house and washing dishes. Later on they do their marketing."

Behind Margo the door opened. Margo wheeled her bulk, hurried away. Regan heard her speaking Spanish with some women. He hobbled out to the store. Five Mexican housewives had entered. They had shopping bags.

For the rest of the day, he and Margo were busy. By evening, the shelves had been strongly depleted, and Regan had a boxful of money. Margo wore a worried look.

"Our stock will not last long at this rate. We will need more stock, Senor Regan."

Old Wad looked funny with a white apron draped the length of his short skinny body. "Another trip to El Paso," he said. "Take a good week there and back. We'd best make tracks tomorrow, Jim."

Jim thought of his small bank account. Would he have enough money to pay for another freight-train of supplies? Maybe he could borrow some credit from the El Paso wholesale house?

"By the time you get back, all this will be sold," Margo said. "And all the money will be in the bank, Senor Regan."

Regan glanced at her. Was she reading his mind?

That afternoon he made the rounds of the mining offices. There was no freight to haul either in or out of Silver City, not even at reduced rates. He hobbled in and talked with Matthew Valenzuela. The merchant was in an empty store, his three clerks acting busy with dustcloths. Regan thought for a while the man would throw him out, Valenzuela was so angry.

"You'll go broke," he threatened.

Regan shrugged. "I'm the one to go bankrupt," he reminded.

He came back to his office and sat down. He was facing the same blank wall in regards to freighting—there was none. Next morning, perched on his high wagon seat, he sent his mules out of Silver City. Behind him trailed a wagon driven by Old Wad, then one by Morrison, then the other came along. The wagons were lashed together, two in an outfit, and eight mules to each set of wagons. Each wagon had a case of dynamite lashed to its reaches.

Regan had a wry thought. If one case went off accidentally, there'd be only a big hole in the desert, nothing more. Regan smiled grimly.

Enrico skinned the fourth lay-out. Johnson, Carlos and Matthew rode saddle-horses, the outside guard. The wagons were empty. The town stood and watched them leave. Maria watched from the window of New Mexico Wagons. Regan saw her slowly lift her hand. He nodded back and took his eyes from her. He had to.

Juan de Cordova had sent six teams out an hour before. He too had two wagons lashed together with log chains. He was hauling out some raw ore that would be refined in El Paso. With it he had two wagons filled with broken mining machinery, bound out of El Paso for repairs back east. His wagons had lumbered slowly, weight heavy on greased axles. Regan's wagons moved faster because they were empty.

They came down the long grade onto the floor of the desert. Because of their heavy loads, here Juan de Cordova had had to rough-lock his wheels, but because their wagons were empty, Regan's men did not have to use heavy-log chains.

Regan shifted his leg, letting his mules have their own way, and looked south, across the endless stretch of desert. The land moved out, grey gravel and brown sand, dunes in the distance, and beyond the tawny sand-dunes the dim, low mountains of blue scarp beyond Lordsburg, marking the International Border.

From the top of the hill, he had been able to see the freighters of New Mexico Wagons, there on the desert floor below, giant ants toiling southeast toward El Paso. But, once on the desert bottom, the wagons were hidden from sight in the endless lift of the land, and could not be seen.

Each of Regan's skinners had hay and ground barley in his wagon, and each had a barrel of water tied on behind the end-wagon, the barrel sitting on the tail-gate, lashed by rope to the wagon, canvasses tied over their tops to keep the precious water from splashing out.

On each side rode the scouts, rifles across their saddles, eyes on the horizon. Regan could not imagine Apaches hitting empty wagons or wagons laden with broken machinery and heavy unrefined ore. Apaches would hit wagons that carried grub and rifles and other supplies necessary to carry on their violent desert raids. But still, a man had to have guards out.

They made an hour camp for noon. He unbandaged his wound and put new bandages on it. The wound was healing nicely. They took the trail again and this time he rode scout, letting the Swede, Johnson, take over the wagons. They caught and passed the Juan de Cordova wagons at three. Regan had the empty wagons and according to freighter-etiquette it was his job to swing wide which he did. Gradually his unladen wagons inched past the heavy wagons of New Mexico Wagons.

Juan de Cordova was out riding scout. Regan could see him on a sorrel horse about half-a-mile to the west. He was glad the man was not skinning a wagon. He wanted no harsh words with de Cordova at this time. His mind was too filled with Maria de Cordova.

He wondered if he had done wrong in taking her in his arms back in his office. Maybe he had given in merely to a whim? Maybe the desire of a healthy young male for a healthy young female had overcome him? He smiled with a quiet humor. He was only lying to himself, he knew. Actually, he should be happy, realising his good luck at winning such a girl as Maria, but he was not happy. His sky had dark foreboding clouds.

What if he killed Juan de Cordova?

His blood ran cold. Maria would leave him then. She could never spend the rest of her life—be the wife of the man who had killed her only brother. That man could not be the father of her children.

Or if Juan de Cordova killed him?

There was no mirth in this thought, either. When a man died the world ended . . . for him, at least. Regan realised his thoughts were dark. But the problem had to be faced. How would he face it, in what manner? Would he leave Silver City?

He shook his head. He would not leave. Maria or no Maria, he'd stay—he would either make a success in Silver City, go broke, or be buried there. And even as these thoughts ran through him, his heart and body were sick.

At four, they met the Silver City bound stage, rocking on its leather through-braces. Regan waved his wagons off-trail and the stage thundered by, six grey horses streaked with sweaty dust, the driver snapping his whip in thanks and recognition. Then it was gone, dust boiling behind it, as it dipped from sight in a wide arroyo that held pale ghost-trees and scraggly green greasewood.

Again there were just his wagons and the silent brooding desert.

They reached Tres Cabezas Springs at five. The springs were almost dry. Green water lay hot and sickly against blue shale. Here New Mexico Wagons had two big galvanised water tanks. These were filled from the spring when it had water.

Soon the spring would be dry, awaiting the short rainy season, which should come in a few months. Juan de Cordova, because of the tanks, would have water, but Regan's outfit would have to carry water, as it now did.

For the next eighty miles there was no water. The next water would be on the bend of the Rio Grande, below old Mesilla.

Juan de Cordova also had built *ramadas*. His crew had cut down scrub cedar, put the posts in the ground, and over these had laid tules and rushes and greasewood. This made an area of shade for his men. Here also he had bales of alfalfa hay, protected from jackrabbits by a woven-wire fence. Until Regan built similar *ramadas* he'd have to tote hay with him.

There was no grass around Tres Cabezas because of the low amount of water in the springs and because New Mexico Wagons mules had grazed it down. Regan knew that Juan de Cordova and his rigs would bed down at the springs. He did not want to meet de Cordova. He was not running from the man, but if he stayed at the springs for the night, crews would mix, and anything could happen—a peaceful night or a gangfight.

They unhitched, watered, fed mules for an hour, then pushed on again, dusk coming across the desert. The night would be a chilly one. That was the way of the desert at this time of the year—hot and blistering by day, ice cold by night.

There was no moon. The night was very dark. Regan called a halt at eleven.

They circled their wagons and unhitched. They watered the mules and threw hay on the sand. Two scouts went out. Regan slept two hours; he awakened stiff, surly.

He and Old Wad took guard. They circled the camp wide, slouched in saddles, bone-weary.

Old Wad spoke once. "How's the leg?"

"All right. No pain."

Dawn came grudgingly. They hitched and resumed plodding. The next two days were the toughest days. They drove mules straight through, stopping for only an hour at noon, sundown, midnight and dawn. Morning of the third day brought them to the bend of the Rio Grande. The Rio Grande was a dirty ribbon of brown water moving lazily between sand dunes.

Outside of each other, the only other people they'd seen in those two days were the few passengers on the stages—and New Mexico Wagons' stages held few passengers due to Apache menace.

Regan was aware of tense rigidity. His eyes never ceased moving across the horizon. All his life he had freighted through Indian country, and this wariness was bred into his sinews.

It was the secret wariness of a man who'd lived always on the rim of civilisation, the border line where White melted into Red. Freighting between Deadwood and Fort Laramie had been the same. Only those Indians had not been Apache; they'd been Cheyenne and Sioux. And the Laredo—San Antonio run had been the same. Again, not Apaches; the plains Comanches.

Always a skinner rode his high seat with a Winchester or Sharps brushing his leg. Always a scout out riding far perimeters.

Always the eternal vigilance.

Upon that vigilance depended their lives.

They'd seen not a sign of Apaches. No horsemen on far sand dunes, no tracks left by recent war-ponies. Only the far reaches of the desert, devoid of animal life except for occasional grey-brown jackrabbits, kangaroo rats, pack rats and a few rattlesnakes.

No Apaches.

They let their mules drink sparingly. From here on it would be all down the Rio Grande to the pasture of the Mexican. Mosquitoes hung in dark curtains. They had stingers like icepicks. Regan looked at a mosquito feasting on his hand. He did not stand up on his stinger to drink human blood. Not a malaria mosquito.

They came into the Mexican's farm

at dusk. Dust-covered wagons. Dust-covered men. Grimy dust-covered mules. They unhitched, three mules on pasture, hit the river. They came out clean and brown and glistening, towelling themselves dry on a gravel bar.

"I'm gettin' so damn' tough," Morrison said, "these mosquitoes bend their stingers on my leathery hide."

He laughed. His scar stood out, marring his face. His eyes were reckless.

Regan knew he would hit the flesh-pots that night. He'd take Old Wad with him, if Old Wad would go. Tomorrow, both would groan with hangovers. After supper, Morrison and Old Wad rode toward El Paso. Old Wad came in about two, stumbling over a chair, softly mouthing drunken curses. He was still asleep, mouth open, when Regan awakened, ate, and went to downtown El Paso.

He went directly to the wholesale house.

"How did it go?" the owner asked.

Regan told him. He went directly to the point. He was running a low bank account. The merchant listened quietly. Then he said, "How much credit will you want, Senor Regan?"

"About three thousand, the way I figure."

"That's quite a bit of money."

Regan pointed out that he had paid cash for the first shipment. The merchant pointed out that the check had not cleared the Silver City bank yet. Regan understood. Banker Jaime Lamas was deliberately holding up his check, clearing it slowly, to cause him trouble. Regan then pointed out that his mules were clear, for evidently the check he had given Ramosa for the wagons had not cleared, either. It would be gathering dust in Lamas' bank, on orders of Juan de Cordova.

When he got back to Silver City, he and the Senor Jaime Lamas would have a serious talk, he thought. It would be short . . . but very serious. Meanwhile, he would give the merchant a promissory note for all over three thousand dollars worth of merchandise, the note anchored on his debt-free mules.

"I'll think it over, Senor Regan."

Regan found himself wondering if Juan de Cordova had not given this merchant a rough time. He knew this same merchant sold wholesale to Valenzuela's *Mercado*. Juan de Cordova might have laid down the law to this man. He could imagine de Cordova's strong point. This man Regan is a fly by night. He might be bankrupt tomorrow. He might be a fraud, a cheat, and never intend to pay you. You've had a steady customer in Matthew Valenzuela for many years. Think it over, man. See the light.

Regan said, in exploration, "Senor de Cordova?"

The man's eyes wavered. "I don't understand you," he said slowly.

Regan smiled. "Don't worry, Senor. I'll be in Silver City a long, long time. My store is selling goods hand over fist. I'm making money on large quantity, not high mark-up. But I'm making money, and Valenzuela's *Mercado* is empty."

"Let me do some figuring." The man drummed thin fingers on the counter.

"Would you want an order identical to the first one?"

Regan shook his head. "I want more groceries and less mercantile stuff, not so much dry goods. More grub. I need more beans and more flour. When I left, I was almost out of beans, and had only four barrels of flour left. The drought made for poor gardens for the mine-workers. No beans, Senor."

"You have an order with you?"

Regan dug and came out with an envelope. "It's all in there. I'll lay over today—my mules need a rest. I should give them two days of rest, but my store needs this shipment."

"I'll let you know tomorrow morning."

"Good. And take my advice."

"Yes, and what is it?"

"Don't swallow everything Juan de Cordova tells you."

The merchant visibly stiffened. "I listen to nobody but my good business sense," he said shortly.

Regan spent the rest of the day greasing wagons and brushing down mules. He and the Mexican farmer talked. Children came home from school. Old Wad and the others went down-town in El Paso. Morrison did not come in. Old Wad came back at dusk. Morrison was drunk in a cantina. "Got not one, but three Mexican girls," Old Wad said.

"You sound jealous," Regan said.

"The older you get, the crazier you talk."

"We've been together all my life," Regan pointed out, "so maybe I went loco because of my company."

Old Wad started for the bunkhouse. He stopped and said, "Juan de Cordova just come into town with his wagons. He rode the whole trip through himself. He's got a barn here in town, you know. He'll load up and head out tomorrow sometime, I guess. We should do the same thing. Get this man here to board half our mules and each time we come down we'll have fresh mules to head home with, like de Cordova."

"The *senor* and I are dickering on that point now." Old Wad shook his head slowly. "I don't get over booze as fast as I used to," he said, and went into the bunkhouse.

Sometime during the night, Morrison and the rest of the crew turned in, smelling of bay-rum, tequilla, stale beer and whiskey. Regan had a bleary-eyed crew at breakfast. When he went into the merchant's office, his heart hammered steadily. Perhaps Juan de Cordova had had another talk with the merchant? His goose might be cooked.

The man was all business. He had a promissory note drawn on the mules. Regan signed it, saying by this time his goods in Silver City were probably sold out, and his check would be covered. If it were, the promissory note would be torn up, the merchant said.

Regan left the store, breathing with new hope. New Mexico Wagons were pulling out, and he judged they had loaded early. Fresh mules lay against collars. Juan de Cordova rode a sorrel horse that pulled at the bit, rolling the bit's cricket. He glanced at Regan. Their eyes met. Neither man spoke, although Regan stood on the edge of the gravel sidewalk and Juan de Cordova rode so close, Regan could have touched de Cordova's near boot.

All except one of de Cordova's wagons were covered with tarps. The one without a tarp showed it carried two huge rolls of paper. Regan thought, For Joseph Cortinas, and a sour taste was on his tongue. And Cortinas had told him he had had no freight to haul. . . . And New Mexico Wagons did not even run an ad in Cortinas' newspaper. Regan decided, then and there, that Senor Cortinas would get no more advertising from one Jim Regan. If he had handbills printed for his store, he'd get the job done in El Paso. Probably cheaper, too.

Regan rode back to camp. Five hours later they had wagons loaded and were heading back to Silver City. The second day out, they passed the de Cordova wagons. One wagon had popped a reach, and when they swung slowly around the New Mexico Wagons' freighters, Regan saw Juan de Cordova and two others under the wagon.

They'd jacked up the reach and they were chaining a plank over the broken span. Once clear of de Cordova's wagons, Regan's freighters again took the rutted road. The heat was heavy; dust rolled in thick clouds. Regan thought, With this dust the Apaches could see us fifty miles away in this thin desert air.

Old Wad swung in from his trick of scouting. His seamed aged face showed worry. "I don't know," he mumbled, "I don't know, Jim."

"You thinking of Cabazon?"

Old Wad's seamed eyes stared past Regan, across the endless desert. "I know Injuns," he said. "I've freighted all my life with the red bastards breathing down my neck."

"Feel their breath now?" Regan made it a joke.

"That I do, Jim."

Regan asked, "See any sign?"

"Not a hoofmark. Not a rider."

306

Regan spoke sharply. "Then give your imagination a rest."

Old Wad climbed up and took the lines and Regan got the horse and rode out to the west, keeping half-mile or so beyond the wagons. He read the soil and he read the horizon and saw nothing. He mopped his sweaty brow. The desert sun was hot today.

They made only thirty miles a day. Five days then from El Paso to Silver City. The second night out, they camped a mile beyond New Mexico Wagons' water tank. Regan worked on the principal, that, if he did not see Juan de Cordova, there would be no trouble. He was undecided; he remembered Maria's warm arms, the promise of her firm girlish body; the sweet warmth of her lips. He groaned inwardly.

They did not unharness mules. They watered them and tied them to end-gates, and grained and fed them. An hour later, the freighters of New Mexico Wagons pulled around the water tank. You could see them across the desert, thin in the distance. Regan saw that no lights showed around wagons. Apache fear rode on their wagon-seats, too.

He looked at his men. They were bearded again, alkali white on their whiskers, faces gaunt, eyes sunken. They were fighting the desert, distance, time and an unseen danger. He rubbed a rough hand over his own whiskery jaw.

He spent most of the night on guard.

Dawn came, mules were again watered, tugs were hitched, again mules plodded on, wagon wheels grinding sand. Old Wad rode close, said, "Juan de Cordova broke camp right behind us."

Regan merely nodded.

The Silver City-El Paso stage rocked out of dust, swung wide to allow the loaded wagons to remain on the trail. Regan saw only one passenger, a man. Then the stage had bulleted on, six horses running madly, and dust rose up, making him cough.

That night, he and Morrison took the early-morning guard. Morrison looked across the desert. There was a pale moon and many shadows.

Morrison said, "I've heard they're not night fighters."

Regan said nothing.

"Something about their Manitou. A fight started in the dark never is successful, or some bull like that. So they hit at dawn and have the whole day ahead of them."

"You're cheerful," Regan said.

The fourth night out, they made camp a mile beyond Tres Cabezas. The mudhole was dry. Juan de Cordova would have to water from his tank there. Regan's crew was scraping water from the bottom of the barrels. The mules would have scanty water tomorrow.

"Be a long dry drag," Old Wad said.

Regan gave no reply. He was afraid he might snap at the old freighter. By late afternoon they should be pulling into Silver City. From here on in the grind would be stiffer, harder on mules and men, for the altitude lifted. They put mules into places, and wheels ground again.

Regan rode scout. From a sand dune, he saw the wagons of New Mexico Wagons stringing out, about a half-mile behind. Then he saw something else too —something mysterious, something awesome. Over a far dune, about a mile west, they came—riders trooping into the dawn, heading for the wagon trains.

His heart froze momentarily. His heart stopped beating. For a long moment he watched in awesome silence. They came over the sand dune then spread out, and he guessed at a hundred warriors, at the least. And there still might be others behind the dune.

His eyes swung east. There they were, too, coming over another low gravel hill. A man came loping up. One of the guards riding for New Mexico Wagons.

The guard pulled his horse to a plunging stop. But when he leaned from saddle, his voice was low and tough.

"Apaches," he said.

"I see them."

He was a short, heavy-set man, and now he stood on his stirrups, glancing first to the west, then the east. His eyes came back to Regan.

"Over two hundred, I'd guess."

"Maybe closer to three," Regan said.

"No use running," the man said. "Our mules are tired. They'd ride along side and get us one by one."

Regan said, "I'll pull in a half circle. Get de Cordova to come in and complete the circle."

The man turned his horse sharply and loped back to the oncoming wagons of Juan de Cordova.

15

MORRISON threw back his head and laughed, white teeth glistening. "What a hell of a hell-to-do! Our wagons tied to them of Juan de Cordova. You an' him'll have a bigger fight inside the circle 'tween yourselves than us boys'll have with them Apaches outside!"

"Get moving!" Regan snapped.

Standing on his seat, blacksnake whip lashing, Old Wad was already swinging the lead wagon off the trail, mules laboring in collars. Regan galloped close, hollered, "Just half a circle. De Cordova's going to build the other half."

"I heard you, damn it!"

Regan pulled his horse out of the dust and loped past his last wagon. His two other outriders came in, horses sweaty. "They're trying to cut in between us and de Cordova," one said.

Regan said, "We can't let them do that."

He loped forward, rifle to his shoulder. He saw an Apache leave his horse, and then the others wheeled and rode back beyond rifle range. Now the lead team of Juan de Cordova's freight train came roaring out of the dust, the driver screaming and popping his blacksnake. Juan de Cordova, riding his big sorrel, came out of the dust, too. Regan saw his grim face, said, "Swing in and complete the circle."

Juan de Cordova's dark eyes swung over to him. For a moment anger ranged across them and then de Cordova said, "Our only chance, I guess."

Regan moved his horse close. "Don't do it unless you want to. I'm willing to fight them in two camps."

"We'd never win," Juan de Cordova said huskily. "Whether we like it or not, Regan, we got to work together."

"That's more like it."

Regan rode around the circle. "Cut mules loose, take them into the ring, throw them and tie them down. We can't have mules stampeding through us. Lash those wagons' tongues to tail-gates."

Men leaped from high seats, rifles in hand, and went to work in the rolling ugly dust. Regan loped back to where Juan de Cordova sat looking at the Apaches. The Apaches were in a long line, one on each side of the circled wagons. Juan de Cordova frowned. "You ever fight redskins before?"

"Not Apaches. Cheyennes, Sioux. Comanches."

Juan de Cordova frowned. "There's something wrong."

Two Apaches rode out of the line on the west. One carried his rifle high, with a white handkerchief tied on to its barrel. They rode straight for the wagons.

"They must want to talk," de Cordova said.

Regan stood on stirrups and spoke to his men. "We're riding out, but not beyond rifle range. Keep your rifles on them."

One was a short middle-aged buck. He

rode a pinto horse bareback. He was naked to the waist. He wore old levis and moccasins. The other was a tall, young Indian, somewhere in his early thirties, Regan guessed. Plainly he was the leader of the two.

Regan said, "Hold up. We're far enough."

The two rode until only fifteen feet separated white from red. Regan said, "That's far enough," and the two halted.

The young one spoke. "You have two men we want." His English was good, Regan noticed—reservation school.

Regan saw a wide, broad nose, marked by smallpox. The face was broad, too, with thick lips, almost negroid. The teeth were almost gone, apparently eaten out by tobacco, and only a few brown fangs remained.

"Who are you?" Regan asked.

"I am Victorio."

Regan saw Juan de Cordova glance at him. Juan de Cordova's face was sweaty, dust clinging to his cheekbones.

"Who do you want?" Regan asked.

"I have ways of finding out names." Victorio spoke slowly. "One man is named Morrison. The other is called Regan."

"Why do you want these two men?"

"They killed my blood brother. His name was Cabazon. He was the man with the ugly head."

"I've heard of him," Regan said.

"These two men did not kill Cabazon fair. Then they did not bury him like a warrior should be buried. I have been told his head hangs on a spike in Silver City." Victorio's eyes bored into Regan's. "I have heard them describe this man Regan. You are the same as he is."

"I'm Regan."

Anger flooded the dark eyes, and Regan tightened his grip on his pistol. For a moment he thought Victorio would lunge from horse at him, meet him in man-to-man conflict.

"We have rifles on you," Regan said, "and the first one that moves, dies."

He saw the older Apache glance toward the wagons.

Now Juan de Cordova spoke in clipped words. "What will you do if we deliver Regan and Morrison to you?"

"We will ride on. We will not touch anybody else." Juan de Cordova looked at Regan. Regan's eyes met de Cordova's. Regan said in Spanish, "It's a hell of a temptation, isn't it, de Cordova? It appeals to your black heart."

Anger touched de Cordova's cheekbones. He said, also in Spanish, "You must take me for a complete fool."

Regan laughed hoarsely. "Hell, you'd do it, de Cordova. Only one thing holds you back."

Victorio cut in with, "Talk words that I know."

Neither Regan or de Cordova paid Victorio any attention.

Juan de Cordova's eyebrow lifted. "What holds me back?"

"You don't trust this red killer. You don't believe him when he says he'll ride on without fighting."

Juan de Cordova laughed soundlessly. "Sometimes I really think you are crazy,

Regan, besides being bullheaded. Do you think I could feed a white man—any man —over to these bastards to stake on an ant-hill?"

Regan said, *"Gracias."*

Juan de Cordova said to Victorio. "We have the men Regan and Morrison. We have twenty other men, too. We have rifles and powder and water and supplies. You'll have to take these two men."

Victorio glanced toward the wagons. Indecision played across his face, giving it a bestial look.

Old Wad hollered, "We've heard every word so far, Jim. I got my Winchester on him with the hammer back. If he makes a move I'm shooting him from that horse. When you leave, turn your horse to the south, so you won't block my sights!"

"We respect your white flag," Regan said. "Turn your horses and go."

Victorio said, "I'll kill you, Regan. And I'll kill Morrison, too. He was my brother."

"You've said that before."

The older buck made a flat gesture,

palm down, and both turned their horses, backs to Regan and Juan de Cordova, and rode away at a walk, not hurrying, taking their time, and Regan guessed at the courage it took to make that ride.

He and Juan de Cordova rode silently back to the circle of wagons.

Old Wad had dropped a wagon-tongue. Regan and de Cordova rode in through the space between the two wagons. Men were throwing mules and tying them in the ring of wagons. They worked quickly. One put a short rope around both of a mule's forelegs, pulled, the mule went down, the hind legs were tied, the mule trussed.

They worked with sweaty, terrible hurry.

Regan said, "Get shovels. Get that dynamite off those reaches. Dig holes for it. One bullet hit a case of that powder, and we'll all be shaking hands with the devil in hell."

Juan de Cordova said, "I don't like that dynamite."

"Like it or don't like it," Regan said shortly. "It's here."

Dust hung in clouds. The Apaches were unhorsed, horses behind the dunes, the warriors prone on the ground. They seemed to be shooting with some sinister intent, spacing shots. Regan looked at a water-barrel. Water spurted from it.

"Get those water barrels off, pronto. They're shooting holes in them, the bastards."

He and Juan de Cordova wrestled barrels, cutting them free. A bullet hit a wagon, making a dull sound. All the mules were down now, lying on their sides, some struggling to rise, others giving up. The wind moved in, hot and searing, sweeping away the dust. The cases of dynamite were not tied to wagon reaches now.

"We ain't got time to dig," Morrison hollered. "Hide that dynamite behind mules."

"Just as good," Regan said.

Juan de Cordova said, "I'll boss the east side, Regan." He belly-crawled

320

through mules, shoving his rifle ahead of him.

Regan crouched behind a wagon's high rear wheel. Old Wad crawled over. "They got the Swede," he said. "He caught a lucky bullet. Right through his heart, Jim."

Regan could only nod.

"They got about half the water," Old Wad continued. "We might be able to get a runner out come dark."

"Sixteen hours away," Regan said.

Old Wad's scrawny fingers grabbed Regan's forearm. Regan looked down on a wrinkled, seamed old face. "Reminds me of the time we turned back the Cheyennes on Little Bear. God almighty, that seems a long time ago, Jim."

"About three years."

"If we did get a runner out, do you think they'd come from Silver City?"

Regan thought of Silver City. At least twenty-five miles away, bound with fear, a makeshift militia marching and shifting rifles. "I don't know," he said. "But I know one thing—we'd never get a man through."

Old Wad squinted at the sun. "This is going to be a hell of a hot day." He squirmed away.

A bullet hit a mule. It made a thudding sound, like a man hitting a small drum. The mule tried to kick. He raised his head, blood coming from his nostrils. He held his head erect, eyes protruding like huge brown glass balls, and for a moment he remained that way, head rigid, neck rigid, body rigid. Then his muscles broke, and his head fell with a thud.

Morrison belly-crawled over, inching around mules. "That de Cordova's crazy," he chuckled. "Damn it, I think he likes this. There's no give to that bastard. He got one as far off as a man could see, wigglin' between two sand dunes."

Regan glanced at him. The jagged scar showed harshly against the whiskery face. Morrison's eyes were evil dark pools.

Both stared west across the desert. They couldn't see much. The greasewood was not thick, but it covered the gravel well. Small gravel-covered dunes rose in small undulant swells. A man's vision was severely limited. They had to shoot while they moved from one hummock to the other, and they were moving very little.

"They don't rush like the Sioux," Morrison said. "They don't wheel in like the Comanches. They just flop out in that damn' sand covering by that greasewood and wait."

"They got the water," Regan said. "We haven't." He shot once. Morrison squinted. "I never saw one move."

"I never got him," Regan said.

Morrison said, "Stages will come in. They might see what's going on, turn around and get word out."

The day wore on. There was spasmodic firing from both sides. The sun arched higher. It held broiling heat. It seared the earth, smashed into the sand, blistered the desert. There was no wind. Morrison established himself as keeper of the water barrels. Men crawled in, he rationed water; he looked into his barrels, and he cursed God and Fate and the entire universe, mostly Apaches.

Carlos sat in the shade, back against a wagon wheel. He coughed with deep and wracking harshness. Regan crept to him. The Mexican had blood on his bare chest, blood that mingled with grimy sweat. The bullet hole was small on the left side of his rib cage. Regan wiped the blood gently away with the back of his hand. The bullet hole was blue, and blood inched out again, driving away the blueness.

Carlos said, "It doesn't take much to kill a man. A little hole in him, and his blood comes out, and his blood breaks loose inside of him. God is good to some men, for God lets them die fast." He crossed himself slowly, and Regan grabbed his arm, fingers severe.

Carlos' wide dark-skinned face was clear. "God had been good to me," he said slowly. "I have had the privilege to live in his clean good world. I had a wonderful wife. She died, and I have my daughter now."

Regan waited, heart beating heavily.

"I have not seen Consuelo for three years. She is with my brother and his wife. She is going to school. I am not afraid to die. I am a part of God, and soon I shall be with Him."

Regan said quietly, "Lie down and let me look at you closer." Carlos shook his head. "There is no use, *Senor* Regan. I will drink a little water and then be with God."

Regan held the tin cup to his lips. The water was very hot. Carlos only wet his lips.

"No more?" Regan asked gently.

"Water is for the living, not the dead. You will need every drop we have. Now go to your work, please."

Regan's eyes searched the dark-skinned face. Carlos smiled at him suddenly, wrinkles forming around his eyes, white teeth showing. Carlos said, "I shall pray you live, *Senor* Regan."

Regan's throat was too congested. He could not answer.

"I have seen the *Senorita* Maria look at

you when you did not see her. And her eyes were the eyes of a woman who looks at the man she wants to be father of her children. My wife always looked at me that way. Now please, *Senor* Regan, go, and let me alone with God."

Regan crept back to his old position.

Morrison said huskily, "He talks of God. Christ, there is no God, or why in the hell would He put us in such a situation? God, hell!" Morrison spat, a small boy showing toughness he did not own.

A few minutes later, Regan glanced toward Carlos. He had toppled onto his side, and he lay very still. Deer flies were gathering around him, sneaking into his gaping mouth.

Regan tore off his shirt. He crept over and put the shirt over Carlos' head. He did not return to his old position beside the wagon wheel. He wormed over to where Juan de Cordova squatted behind a wagon wheel, his Winchester poked between the spokes, the hub shielding him.

"We're in a tight spot," de Cordova said.

"Any damn' fool knows that."

Juan de Cordova looked at him. Hell blazed across his dark eyes. Then it left before his smile.

"Regan, you're a hell of a guy. You come into town, shake the hell out of me, and I sit there and wonder, 'What the hell is wrong with this loco gringo.'"

Regan watched him. Juan de Cordova still smiled. "Then you trail in mules, beat the hell out of Morrison, and you and Morrison make that Mogollon run two gringo fools with guts made of brass."

"You complimenting me? Or are you condemning me?"

Juan de Cordova's breath rasped hoarsely. "Still the fool gringo, eh? Now I can see why you used dynamite."

"We've got some more," Regan pointed out.

"But how to get it out to them?" Juan de Cordova squinted out across the desert with its shifting greasewood shimmering in the liquid heat of the sun. "Run out there like a boy taking candy to his teacher? 'Here, Mister Victorio. A present for you. A stick of dynamite to blow you to hell!' That the way, Regan?"

"That would be about it."

Juan de Cordova's lips grimaced. "You might have the answer, at that," he said, and shot. "Hell, I missed him a country mile. How's the ammunition holding out?"

"I always haul a couple of cases of cartridges when I move. Sioux taught me that up north. How about your wagons?"

"Not too much," Juan de Cordova said.

Noon came. The sun became even hotter. Flies came swarming in, buzzing and bloodthirsty. Mules lay silently, giving up. Morrison crept from man to man with his bucket of cold beans. Greasewood and *chamisal* shimmered in the intense heat. Dunes of gravel and sand were ghost-like lines criss-crossing the parched earth.

The northbound stage came in at three-fourteen by Regan's watch. The Apaches cut it off a half-mile south, driving it west off the trail, and they could hear sharp yips, and they shot, but the distance was far. Juan de Cordova did bring down a horse, though. It skidded on its side, throwing its almost naked rider, who darted into the brush.

The stage rocked into an arroyo and out of sight. After a while, a thin column of smoke arose from the coulee.

The southbound stage came in at four-twenty. The Apaches tried to cut it off a mile from the wagons, but the driver drove through. He stood on his platform, lashing his horses; they reared on, Apaches closing in. But the stage got through, and the Apaches fell back, not moving into accurate rifle range.

The driver was gone now, falling back in the greasewood, but the six horses ran wildly. They came smashing in, crashed into a wagon, and there was a dust-rolling mess of horses, wagons, and stage. The tongue broke, freeing the horses, and they stampeded to the east, one horse falling, then being jerked to his feet, and they went out of sight behind a sand dune, leaving the stage. The stage had a broken high front wheel, and it rested against a wagon.

Morrison said, "By God, if he had any passengers, he sure gave them a ride."

Nobody came out of the stage. Regan could not see its windows because the freight wagon was in the way.

Somebody said, "We're getting company!"

Two hundred yards away, the stage-driver came on the run, zig-zagging through the brush, geysers of gravel spurting around him. He was a heavy man, and they built up a barrage to cover him. He was twenty feet from the wagons when he slumped ahead, lost a stride, and landed on his belly, head bent under him.

"Well," Morrison said dryly, "he tried, poor devil."

Regan raised up slightly and studied the fallen man. He watched him for some moments. The driver did not move. He just lay there, head cocked at a sharp angle. Regan settled back.

"Guess he had no passengers," Morrison said.

Regan settled down again. He shot occasionally, but he knew their game—play it close, get them one by one, let the sun and lack of water do their deadly sentence. He was impatient, he wanted to hit, to strike, to drive them back; he wanted no more of this terrible sun, this gravel under his belly, no more of death.

Morrison made a slow survey of the enclosure. When he came back, an hour later, he said, "There were seventeen of us to start with. Juan had ten and we had seven."

"How many now?"

"Twelve."

"You count the mules?"

"Six dead." He paused. "We haven't got many teams to get these wagons out of here." He rubbed his scar. "That is, if we ever get out."

Morrison reached out. He laid his hand

on Regan's forearm. A smile split his whiskers.

Regan listened.

"It's a hell of a cockeyed world. I remember when I was in the sixth grade. We had a teacher whose face would stop a sevenday clock. Old Lady Benson, her name was. We were reading about the Thirty Year War. The world was going to hell then. It's still going to hell. But it sure gets there in a slow hurry!"

"Give us time," Regan said. "We'll make it."

Old Wad called, "Hell, I think there's somebody in that stage. Seems to me like I heard a voice in it."

Regan crept over to where the old freighter was stationed. There was no sound now from the stage. Regan bellied under the wagon, got the stage's door open, and looked inside.

The woman lay on the floor. She had a cut on her forehead. Her dark eyes looked into his less than two feet away. He saw glistening black hair. He said, "Can you crawl out?"

Her eyes held a stunned look. "What happened?"

"The driver crashed the stage."

She did not move. She said, "I remember the Apaches jumping us. I bounced ahead and hit something." Her small hand came up and touched her forehead, and she brought it down and looked at the blood. "I guess I got knocked unconscious." Suddenly fear tore across her eyes. "Juan?" It was more than one word. It was a prayer.

"He's still alive."

She said, "I was running away. I was running from him and our problem. But I didn't run away. I ran right back into the problem."

Regan said, "Don't talk."

He pulled her from the aisle. "Now keep your body low. Creep under the wagon. Juan is over across on the other side."

"What shall I tell him?"

"I don't know, Senorita Beauvrais. That is up to you, is it not?" He looked beyond her into the stage. A fat man lay in the aisle on his back, head bent queerly on one side. Regan recognised him as a salesman he'd seen in Silver City. When alive the salesman's face had been red with broken blood vessels from excessive drinking. Now the face was pale, the jowls sagging and the color of dead fish.

"Just you two?" Regan asked.

A bullet hit the wagon over them. It made a dull plucking sound. Madame Beauvrais ducked. Regan did not.

"Just we two."

Regan said, "Creep between the mules. They won't kick you. They're tied all four feet. Don't show an inch of your body."

Juan de Cordova called, "What's going on over there?"

Regan left her and inched back to where Morrison sat. Morrison laughed with shaky humor. "The plot thickens, Regan. The concubines come home to roost. Be hell of a way for a woman to die. You know, those devils are coming in closer. About sundown the curtains are goin' be jerked shut." He laid his cheek against the stock of his rifle and took deliberate aim and fired. "I think I at least made him jump. You know, they seem to be congregating more on our side. I guess the other side must have better shots, huh?"

Regan thought of Maria. He remembered her softness, the light of her eyes, the feel of her against him—God, he thought, Oh, God, I'm not going to die, am I? There was no answer, but he felt a lift within him.

Ten minutes later he was lying beside Old Wad when the bullet hit the old man in the chest. Wad rose a little, turned his head and looked at him, and then went down on his belly, only his fingers moving slightly, and then they were still, too.

Regan had a confused thought, The old don't have much life. We buried your father in Old Mexico, Regan. Your mother in Texas. But where will you bury Old Wad? And outside, the spring sun had touched the beautiful Black Hills of South Dakota, coaxing the hills into green life.

I know now, he thought.

A mule raised his head. He whinnied, tried to kick his trussed legs. His head dropped. He regarded Regan with warm brown eyes. Regan saw blood on the mule's back.

He wormed his way to where Juan de Cordova sat, legs out in front of him, rifle still balanced on the wagon spoke.

"Where's the woman?"

"She's taking care of Matthewson. He got one in his lungs." Juan de Cordova loaded his rifle with trembling hands, but his jaw was solid granite. "She was running, Regan. She was running away from me."

"What else could she do?"

Juan de Cordova's eyes bored into his. "She didn't have to run. I'd have taken her. Maybe I've learned something today. Sure, she used to be a whore, until she met me. Then she had attention for nobody but me. You meet a woman, Regan. You know nothing about her. You love her, you marry her—and because you know nothing about her, maybe she'd been a whore, too, but you never know, so you thought nothing about it—because she never told you."

Regan had no answer.

Juan de Cordova breathed deeply, nostrils flaring. He caught himself. Regan said, "Old Wad is dead. Both stages are wrecked. No word will get through. We got to use black powder."

"I understand why you and Morrison used dynamite, now."

Regan hollered, "All of you. Listen. Meet in the middle. Among the mules. Morrison, bring dynamite."

"Best words I've heard all day," Morrison called back.

Nine of them gathered there and one was a woman. She had blood on her forehead, blood on her black silk dress, and she had her hand over that of Juan de Cordova, and her dark eyes were not on the dynamite, but on the sweat streaked dirty face of Juan de Cordova.

"I know dynamite," one of Juan de Cordova's men said. "I worked in the mines. I can fit the caps."

Morrison worked with fuses and caps.

"Regan showed me how," he said. "But hell, I knew before he showed me."

Regan worked, too, and as he worked he talked. "Five sticks to a man. Put them in our belts. First we lay out a barrage, Victorio is on the west, I think. We hit the west, five of us."

"What about the other four?" Morrison asked.

"When we hit the west side, they'll come in from the east. Four stay here and meet them with black powder as they rush in."

Morrison said, "I want to move. I want to kill the bastards. I want the west."

Juan de Cordova said, "I'll take that, too."

Regan looked at his two men, Matthew and Enrico. Matthew said, "We're with you, Jim."

Regan looked at Madame Beauvrais. "You stay here and help the men." He noticed her free hand held a pistol. He said no more to her.

"We got the sticks ready," Morrison said. He loosened his gunbelt and shoved five sticks under it. "Bullet hit me in the belly and there'll be a hell of a hole in the sand." His scar stood out lividly.

"Line up on the west side," Regan ordered. "Get about twenty feet apart, or around there. When I holler, throw out your first stick. Throw it as far as you can."

He looked at Morrison. The man was grinning, cock-sure. Juan de Cordova's handsome face was tense. Short Matthew had a blunt dead face. Enrico's eyes held tears. Regan wondered how he looked. Like the wrath of hell, he thought.

"Just as soon as the powder explodes we advance. We get to the crater holes and we throw out again. From then on, God knows."

Juan de Cordova crossed himself. Enrico also crossed himself. Matthew said, "Let God be with us. God, look down on us, and give us your Divine Help."

Morrison said, "T'hell with God. Let's start moving. I depend more on my arm and dynamite."

They stationed themselves. Regan said, "Matches lit." He paused a moment, lighting his own match. "Matches to fuses. All right, now stand up, and throw!"

The sticks arced in the air. They sped out, hit the gravel, and then roared gravel skyward. Five men leaped over wagon tongues, running, holding rifles, running forward, and Matthew stopped suddenly, slumping ahead. They ran through dust. They saw little but dust. Then Regan saw a huge hole ahead, he hit and hollered, "Matches again. Fuses. Throw, damn you, throw!"

Again, dynamite went out, sputtering, arcing. Again the earth trembled. Again, men moved forward, only four this time. From then on, all was confusion.

Something hit Regan across the shoulders. At first he thought he'd been shot. Then he saw it was a leg, torn loose at the thigh, that had smashed into him.

The leg almost knocked him down. He rolled, came into another pit left by dynamite, somehow lit another match. He threw the dynamite the way a man throws a hand-grenade. It hit the ground, roared, and a head smashed on the ground beside him. The jaw broke loose, rolled one direction, the head the other.

An Apache came out of the dust. He had a knife in his teeth and a rifle. Regan shot him through the chest. The Apache went down, fired once, and broke Regan's left arm, below the elbow.

"They're running for their horses!" The hoarse voice belonged to Morrison. "Shoot them down."

He could see Morrison now, about thirty feet away. Morrison saw him, too. Morrison turned to holler something. His mouth opened, but he said nothing. The bullet hit him on the scar. Morrison fell without a sound.

Regan fell, hanging onto his rifle. He landed behind a sagebrush. He put his rifle over it and shot. He got two Apaches, and then somebody threw more dynamite, and all was dust again. But there was no returning fire; at least, none at him.

Behind him, he heard dynamite explode. He sat up, looked at the wagons, saw the dust billowing. skyward on the east. They had made their break in from that direction. Even as he watched, he saw Apaches running, heading for horses. Dynamite came into the group. A man caught it, went to throw the stick back, but it exploded over the Apaches. The next thing Regan saw was dust, and after the dust, an empty hole in the desert.

There was no shooting now any place. There was only dust and the wind was moving it away. He staggered to the summit of a hummock of sand. The Apaches were heading out, riding in a fast swirl of dust, going southeast. Regan thought, This is the way hell will be, I guess.

The Apaches fell from sight in an arroyo. He looked south. The other bunch were swinging wide, intending to join their fellows in the southwest. They too fell from sight.

The world was quiet. Very, very quiet. The sun burned down. He looked about him. He felt sick. He remembered reading about Shiloh. The bodies lay there, the blue and the grey, the newspapers had said, and they lay together, enemy and foe, together. . . . Only this was Red and White, not Blue and Grey.

Juan de Cordova was on his knees, hands over his belly. Blood was on his fingers. He raised a white, dust-streaked face.

"We're the only two left?"

"The only two."

"Your arm is broken."

Regan sat down beside him. The world spun, tipped on its axis, and then steadied. He got de Cordova on his back. The man was shot through the right side, just above his belt.

"Missed the dynamite," Juan de Cordova said. "I was lucky, Regan. Damn' lucky."

Madame Beauvrais came. She knelt beside Juan de Cordova who said, "Why, hello there, beautiful."

She started to tear off de Cordova's shirt. "Regan," she said, "we got to send

343

a man out. We lost two, back at the wagons."

Regan got to his feet. He looked down at Juan de Cordova who had his eyes closed. Regan turned, stumbled to the wagons. He fell in a pit hole, got up, stumbled on again.

"What's your name?" he asked a de Cordova driver.

The man stared at him oddly. He had come through without a scratch. "What the hell difference does it make?"

"Get a horse," Regan said, "and ride for Silver City."

They came two hours later and they rode like the horde of Genghis Khan, and General Humberto Gonzales headed them in the best revolutionary manner, a huge man on a black thundering horse, with sabre upraised. Regan had to smile. Gonzales was fighting Maximilian again.

They came out of saddles and Humberto Gonzales took charge, and Regan saw disgust move across the face of Sheriff Lucas Garcia. They got the wounded in one wagon they had hurriedly unloaded, got the dead in another, and they moved them toward Silver City. Juan de Cordova lay on the floor of the first wagon, with Madame Beauvrais sitting beside him, the doctor on the other side.

Regan rode with one arm in a sling. He was weak from loss of blood. Maria de Cordova rode beside him. He was aware of her eyes on him.

"I'm worried about you," she said.

Regan said, "You keep on worrying, Maria, and I'll be happy."

Epilogue

JUAN DE CORDOVA died on the route in to Silver City. He called to Jim Regan, and when Regan rode close and looked down, Juan de Cordova said, in soft Spanish, "You're a good man. Take good care of my sister."

They buried him next day, and the woman known as Madame Beauvrais left Silver City that afternoon and never returned.

The doctor amputated Jim Regan's arm, six inches below the elbow. Wrapping reins around the stump, he drove stage for an even thirty years, from 1879 to 1909. That year—1909—rails were laid from Deming to Silver City, and freighting was over forever.

By that time, Regan had built the big

new two-story brick building on Bullard Street, wherein he had his general store and, in 1909, he turned the management of that store over to his oldest child, Sarah, and her husband, Woodrow, and he moved to his rancho on the San Francisco River—the ranch he had built by irrigation, hard work and hopes.

There, in the big sprawling adobe house he built on the mesa, he spent the rest of his life, tending his livestock and working his alfalfa fields, and there he died in 1917, a respected New Mexico pioneer, a man who'd seen the territory become a state. He died suddenly, two weeks before his second boy, Juan, was killed in the First World War, in France.

Jim Regan died at the age of 67.

Six years later, in 1923, his gracious grey-haired wife, Maria, followed him in death, leaving their oldest boy, Matthew, to run the rancho.

Of the union of Maria de Cordova and James Regan, five children were born, two dying before the age of three.

Enrique Williams never found The

Lost Adam. Three years after Regan came to Silver City, Enrique Williams went again into the Mogollon wilderness, and did not return. Twelve years later, hunters found a skeleton of a lone man. Across his canteen in faced letters were the words: Enrique Williams.

The Lost Adam Mine has never been found.

Victorio, the Apache, came out of the battle at Tres Cabezas shattered and shocked, ripped by flying gravel. He never again struck at Jim Regan.

General Crook, the Ute campaign settled in Colorado, came once again to the corner of southwest New Mexico and southeast Arizona, and Victorio was through. Years later when Geronimo flared up on the warpath, the great humanitarian-general, General Nelson Appleton Miles, moved into this territory, and the Apache uprisings were over for all time.

The dust settles.

Lee Floren.

SUNDANCE: SILENT ENEMY
by John Benteen

Both the Indians and the U.S. Cavalry were being victimized. A lone crazed Cheyenne was on a personal war path against both sides. They needed to pit one man against one crazed Indian. That man was Sundance.

LASSITER
by Jack Slade

Lassiter wasn't the kind of man to listen to reason. Cross him once and he'd hold a grudge for years to come—if he let you live that long. But he was no crueler than the men he had killed, and he had never killed a man who didn't need killing.

LAST STAGE TO GOMORRAH
by Barry Cord

Jeff Carter, tough ex-riverboat gambler, now had himself a horse ranch that kept him free from gunfights and card games. Until Sturvesant of Wells Fargo showed up. Jeff owed him a favour and Sturvesant wanted it paid up. All he had to do was to go to Gomorrah and recover a quarter of a million dollars stolen from a stagecoach!

McALLISTER ON THE COMANCHE CROSSING
by Matt Chisholm

The Comanche, deadly warriors and the finest horsemen in the world, reckon McAllister owes them a life—and the trail is soaked with the blood of the men who had tried to outrun them before.

QUICK-TRIGGER COUNTRY
by Clem Colt

Turkey Red hooked up with Curly Bill Graham's outlaw crew and soon made a name for himself. But wholesale murder was out of Turk's line, so when range war flared he bucked the whole border gang alone . . .

PISTOL LAW
by Paul Evan Lehman

Lance Jones came back to Mustang for just one thing—Revenge! Revenge on the people who had him thrown in jail; on the crooked marshal; on the human vulture who had already taken over the town. Now it was Lance's turn . . .

GUNSLINGER'S RANGE
by Jackson Cole

Three escaped convicts are out for revenge. They won't rest until they put a bullet through the head of the dirty snake who locked them behind bars.

RUSTLER'S TRAIL
by Lee Floren

Jim Carlin knew he would have to stand up and fight because he had staked his claim right in the middle of Big Ike Outland's best grass. Jim also had a score to settle with his renegade brother.

Larry and Stretch:
THE TRUTH ABOUT SNAKE RIDGE
by Marshall Grover

The troubleshooters came to San Cristobal to help the needy. For Larry and Stretch the turmoil began with a brawl, then an ambush, and then another attempt on their lives—all in one day.

WOLF DOG RANGE
by Lee Floren

Montana was big country, but not big enough for a ruthless land-grabber like Will Ardery. He would stop at nothing, unless something stopped him first—like a bullet from Pete Manly's gun.

Larry and Stretch: DEVIL'S DINERO
by Marshall Grover

Plagued by remorse, a rich old reprobate hired the Texas Troubleshooters to deliver a fortune in greenbacks to each of his victims. Even before Larry and Stretch rode out of Cheyenne, a traitor was selling the secret and the hunt was on.

CAMPAIGNING
by Jim Miller

Ambushed on the Santa Fe trail, Sean Callahan is saved from dying by two Indian strangers. Then the trio is joined by a former slave called Hannibal. But there'll be more lead and arrows flying before the band join the legendary Kit Carson in his campaign against the Comanches.

DONOVAN
by Elmer Kelton

Donovan was supposed to be dead. The town had buried him years before when Uncle Joe Vickers had fired off both barrels of a shotgun into the vicious outlaw's face as he was escaping from jail. Now Uncle Joe had been shot—in just the same way.

CODE OF THE GUN
by Gordon D. Shirreffs

MacLean came riding home with saddle-tramp written all over him, but sewn in his shirt-lining was an Arizona Ranger's star. MacLean had his own personal score to settle—in blood and violence!

GAMBLER'S GUN LUCK
by Brett Austen

Gamblers hands are clean and quick with cards, guns and women. But their names are black, and they seldom live long. Parker was a hell of a gambler. It was his life—or his death . . .

ORPHAN'S PREFERRED
by Jim Miller

A boy in a hurry to be a man, Sean Callahan answers the call of the Pony Express. With a little help from his Uncle Jim and the Navy Colt .36, Sean fights Indians and outlaws to get the mail through.

DAY OF THE BUZZARD
by T. V. Olsen

All Val Penmark cared about was getting the men who killed his wife. All young Jason Drum cared about was getting back his family's life savings. He could not understand the ruthless kind of hate Penmark nursed in his guts.

THE MANHUNTER
by Gordon D. Shirreffs

Lee Kershaw knew that every Rurale in the territory was on the lookout for him. But the offer of $5,000 in gold to find five small pieces of leather was too good to turn down.

RIFLES ON THE RANGE
by Lee Floren

Doc Mike and the farmer stood there alone between Smith and Watson. Doc Mike knew what was coming. There was this moment of stillness, a clock-tick of eternity, and then the roar would start. And somebody would die . . .

HARTIGAN
by Marshall Grover

Hartigan had come to Cornerstone to die. He chose the time and the place, but he did not fight alone. Side by side with Nevada Jim, the territory's unofficial protector, they challenged the killers—and Main Street became a battlefield.

HARSH RECKONING
by Phil Ketchum

The minute Brand showed up at his ranch after being illegally jailed, people started shooting at him. But five years of keeping himself alive in a brutal prison had made him tough and careless about who he gunned down . . .

FIGHTING RAMROD
by Charles N. Heckelmann

Most men would have cut their losses, but Frazer counted the bullets in his guns and said he'd soak the range in blood before he'd give up another inch of what was his.

LONE GUN
by Eric Allen

Smoke Blackbird had been away too long. The Lequires had seized the Blackbird farm, forcing the Indians and settlers off, and no one seemed willing to fight! He had to fight alone.

THE THIRD RIDER
by Barry Cord

Mel Rawlins wasn't going to let anything stand in his way. His father was murdered, his two brothers gone. Now Mel rode for vengeance.

RIDE A LONE TRAIL
by Gordon D. Shirreffs

The valley was about to explode into open range war. All it needed was the fuse and Ken Macklin was it.

ARIZONA DRIFTERS
by W. C. Tuttle

When drifting Dutton and Lonnie Steelman decide to become partners they find that they have a common enemy in the formidable Thurston brothers.

TOMBSTONE
by Matt Braun

Wells Fargo paid Luke Starbuck to outgun the silver-thieving stagecoach gang at Tombstone. Before long Luke can see the only thing bearing fruit in this eldorado will be the gallows tree.

HIGH BORDER RIDERS
by Lee Floren

Buckshot McKee and Tortilla Joe cut the trail of a border tough who was running Mexican beef into Texas. They stopped the smuggler in his tracks.

HARD MAN WITH A GUN
by Charles N. Heckelmann

After Bob Keegan lost the girl he loved and the ranch he had sweated blood to build, he had nothing left but his guts and his guns but he figured that was enough.

BRETT RANDALL, GAMBLER
by E. B. Mann

Larry Day had the choice of running away from the law or of assuming a dead man's place. No matter what he decided he was bound to end up dead.

THE GUNSHARP
by William R. Cox

The Eggerleys weren't very smart. They trained their sights on Will Carney and Arizona's biggest blood bath began.

THE DEPUTY OF SAN RIANO
by Lawrence A. Keating and
Al. P. Nelson

When a man fell dead from his horse, Ed Grant was spotted riding away from the scene. The deputy sheriff rode out after him and came up against everything from gunfire to dynamite.

SUNDANCE: IRON MEN
by Peter McCurtin

Sundance, assigned to save the railroad from a murder spree, soon came to realise that he'd have to fight fire with fire, bullets with bullets and death with death!

FARGO: MASSACRE RIVER
by John Benteen

Fargo spurred his horse to the edge of the road. The ambushers up ahead had now blocked the road. Fargo's convoy was a jumble, a perfect target for the insurgents' weapons!

SUNDANCE:
DEATH IN THE LAVA
by John Benteen

The land echoed with the thundering hoofs of Modoc ponies. In minutes they swooped down and captured the wagon train and its cargo of gold. But now the halfbreed they called Sundance was going after it, and he swore nothing would stand in his way.

GUNS OF FURY
by Ernest Haycox

Dane Starr, alias Dan Smith, wanted to close the door on his past and hang up his guns, but people wouldn't let him. Good men wanted him to settle their scores for them. Bad men thought they were faster and itched to prove it. Starr had to keep killing just to stay alive.